The Wild Ones

THE SWINGERS 5

The Wild Ones

Nick Clarke

POCKET
B O O K S

New York London Toronto Sydney Tokyo Singapore

First published in Great Britain by
Pocket Books in 1994
A division of Simon & Schuster Ltd
A Paramount Communications Company

Simon & Schuster Ltd
West Garden Place
Kendal Street
London W2 2AQ

Simon & Schuster of Australia Pty Ltd
Sydney

A CIP catalogue record for this book is
available from the British Library

ISBN 0-671-85185-3

Typeset in Times by
Hewer Text Composition Services, Edinburgh
Printed and bound in Great Britain by
HarperCollins Manufacturing, Glasgow

To Sir Louis S*g*l
With Thanks for the Memories

Hypocrisy is the homage paid by vice to virtue.

Duc de la Rochefoucauld (1613–1680)

ONE

Oh, What A Beautiful Morning

It was a surprisingly cold and windy April morning, especially as the first three months of 1966 had been relatively mild, and Ivor Belling's raincoat flapped wildly around his legs as he waited for the change from the ten shilling note he had given to the taxi driver who had just pulled up outside the front door of Cable Publicity in High Holborn.

So although he recognised and was mildly irritated by the stratagem of the driver who was clumsily fumbling about in one pocket after another for shillings, sixpences and threepenny pieces, Ivor told him in a gruff voice to keep the change. He turned away and raised a hand in acknowledgment of the driver's profuse thanks as he opened the door into the warm sanctuary of his company's plush, air-conditioned offices.

Cable Publicity's appetising new auburn-haired receptionist smiled at him as he walked by her desk and called out brightly: 'Good morning, Mr Belling, you're in early this morning.'

Ivor flashed her a slightly wan smile. 'Good morning, Miss Howard, my aren't we formal today.'

The pretty girl laughed and said: 'Sorry, Ivor, force

of habit. My last job was in a solicitor's office where everyone was Mister or Miss whilst you were expected to call the senior partners "sir".'

'I wouldn't have thought that was your scene, Debbie,' he replied as he picked up his mail from the neat piles of letters which the receptionist had stacked up by the switchboard.

'It certainly wasn't, but the pay was good and I saved enough to go on a three-week holiday in Devon after I left,' she explained whilst she proferred a slip of paper across the desk. 'Oh Ivor, Mr Reese – whoops, there I go again! – I mean Martin called about ten minutes ago and left a message for you. Could you please call him at this number at half past eleven?'

Ivor took the paper and murmured: 'Hampstead 2305 . . . now why does this number ring a bell?' and then he let out a low growl as he remembered that it was the home number of Carole, Cable's former receptionist who was now working as a personal assistant to Martin Reese, the managing director of the agency. Carole was a light-skinned West Indian girl, slightly plump but blessed with dark liquid eyes and generous high tilted breasts which jutted out proudly from underneath the tight woollen sweaters she favoured during the winter months.

He chuckled softly as he gleefully recalled the uproarious evening six months before when Martin had taken him to a smart restaurant along with Carole and her attractive friend, Melanie, and then back to his flamboyant boss's luxury flat where the four of them had indulged in some of the wildest group sex Ivor had ever experienced.

Of course, Martin Reese had insisted that Carole's elevation from the reception desk to his office had nothing whatsoever to do with the sultry girl's ability between the sheets. It was rather her quick mind and brisk efficiency which had earned her the promotion – and to be fair to Martin, who never entertained the slightest misgiving about screwing any of the girls who worked for the company, Carole soon showed that she possessed an undoubted ability to organise his often chaotic diary.

'Would you like a cup of tea?' enquired Debbie, breaking his reverie. 'I was just about to put the kettle on.'

'Oh, yes please, milk and one sugar, please,' said Ivor as he pushed open the swing door into the corridor which led to the directors' domain. He climbed the stairs to the second floor (it was his only exercise during the working day) and once inside his office, he threw his mail on the polished mahogany desk. Then he took off his raincoat and walked across to the window to gaze down on the hordes of people scurrying around in the rain. It was only eight fifty-five and he rarely made an appearance more than a few minutes before the official opening time of the office, which was at half past nine.

But last night Ivor had spent the evening at the Hunkiedorie Club entertaining one of his best contacts, a feature writer on the *Daily Sketch*, who could usually be relied upon to file a story which would publicise one of Ivor's accounts, from the pop singer Ruff Trayde to Ronnie Bloom's swimwear or even the Four Seasons dog food on which he had worked so diligently [see *The Swingers 4: Coming Through The Rye*].

Like most newspapermen, Simon Barber enjoyed a drink, but Ivor had made the mistake of accepting Simon's invitation to have a night-cap when the taxi dropped them off outside the journalist's flat. One final brandy would not have caused any problems for Ivor, but at the front door they met Claire and Wendy, two miniskirted young girls from the flat upstairs who had also just arrived home after a night at a club. They had readily agreed to help the men polish off the bottle of fine cognac which Simon had been given the previous week on a 'freebie' trip to the vineyards, and by half past one the couples had paired off and Ivor found himself in Wendy's bedroom, locked in a passionate embrace with the nubile, dark-haired teenager.

As he looked out of the window Ivor smiled wryly as he remembered how sweet and firm Wendy's tongue had tasted as it traced the inside of his lips, and then how it had flashed lightly across to touch his own as he unbuttoned her blouse and slipped his hands inside to cup her pert breasts. In no time at all they had stripped off their clothes and Ivor had slid down the bed and buried his face in the soft mound of black curls between her thighs.

To his delight, Wendy's pussy was already juicy and open and she had cried out with joy as he teased her fleshy clitty with the tip of his tongue. She had struggled up and he had seen her delicious curves gleaming in

4

the moonlight as she straddled him and rubbed her moist love-lips against his knob, before plunging up and down, fucking herself on his throbbing erection whilst he licked and nibbled her hard, red nipples.

Ivor slowly played back the sexy scene in his mind and by the time he moved away from the window and sat down on his deep leather chair, his prick was making a large bulge in his lap and his hand wandered down to squeeze his cock as he wondered how Wendy had managed to time her climax so that it came seconds after he had spurted a fountain of spunk inside her cunt.

Frankly, he would have been quite happy to have gone to sleep there and then but, after a short rest, Wendy had slicked her fist up and down his shaft so sensuously that, to his suprise, he had woken up to find his cock fully erect.

'Take me from behind,' Wendy had whispered as she scrambled to her knees and thrust her rounded bum cheeks into the air, and Ivor had readily obeyed, kneeling up behind her and sliding his shaft into her wet cunny. Summoning up his last reserves of strength, he had begun thrusting in and out of her sopping honeypot with long, deep strokes whilst he reached forward to cup her perky, firm breasts and tease her nipples back to hardness.

He grinned as he recalled how this time Wendy had come first and it had taken almost a dozen full-depth, pile-driving thrusts before he had ejaculated a second stream of sticky seed into her clinging love channel.

Fortunately for Ivor, Wendy had been generous enough to let him set the alarm clock to ring at half past six and, after he had kissed her goodbye and tip-toed out of her bedroom, he had picked up a passing taxi to take him back to his own flat in Hampstead.

After a quick shower, shave and a change of clothes, he had scanned the newspaper as he waited for the bread to pop out of the toaster. The papers were still full of news about Labour's General Election triumph the previous week which had raised Prime Minister Harold Wilson's majority from four to almost one hundred. But what had caught Ivor's eye had been a story in the *Guardian* about how the American magazine *Time* was toasting London as the swinging city of the decade, declaring that 'this spring, as never before in modern times, London is switched on. Ancient elegance and new opulence are all tangled in a dazzling blur. In a once sedate world of faded splendour, everything new, uninhibited and kinky is blooming at the top of London life.'

This was all grist to Ivor's mill because only last week, Cable Publicity had won the account to handle publicity for The Cranbrook, a luxurious new hotel in Mayfair, and favourable press coverage in America would boost the number of tourists, which had to be good news for The Cranbrook and its owner, Andy Edwards, a sharp Cockney entrepreneur who over the last three years had amassed a highly profitable and growing leisure empire.

Again, lady luck had smiled upon him when he decided to get to the office early, for just as he was about to cross Finchley Road to catch the Underground train into town, he spotted a taxi with its meter up crawling in the heavy traffic towards the West End. Sod the expense, he muttered to himself, as he ran towards the cab and flagged down the driver, and once inside the warm, dry cab he relaxed and moulded himself against the soft leather of his comfortable seat and felt more than a twinge of sympathy for the poor buggers squashed against each other in the crowded carriages of the Bakerloo Line.

Ivor really disliked using the tube, for he suffered from a mild claustrophobia when the train stopped in the tunnel between stations, unlike one of his major clients who loved his journeys on the Piccadilly Line during the rush hours, when the passengers were crushed together like sardines and he found himself with countless opportunities to rub his stiff prick against the soft, rounded bodies of the office girls . . .

A knock on the door interrupted his reverie and he walked over to his desk and shouted 'Come in', as Debbie came into his office carrying a mug of tea, which she carefully deposited on a coaster.

'Many thanks, love,' said Ivor as he smiled gratefully at the leggy girl whose light green miniskirt scarcely covered the tops of her stockings. 'Honestly, Debbie, I feel really sorry for you having to struggle in to work so early on such a rotten morning.'

'Well actually I don't mind an early start, and the days are getting longer now we're into spring,' replied Debbie. 'And I do leave early, you know, so I've plenty of time to prepare myself to have fun in the evenings.'

'I promise I'll try not to overload Craig Grey then,' he said teasingly, for Ivor knew that Debbie was dating the handsome young head of Cable's market research department.

However, far from rising to the bait, Debbie simply shrugged her shoulders and declared crossly: 'I wouldn't care if you did, Ivor, I'm very angry with Craig just now and I don't know whether I want to go out with him any more.'

'Oh dear, why not? What's Mr Grey been up to?' asked Ivor, who tried hard (if not always successfully) to resist the temptation to become involved with the girls on Cable's staff. 'Has he been two-timing you?'

'In a manner of speaking, though not with another girl,' said Debbie and Ivor grinned and remarked: 'Gosh, he's not on the turn, is he? I can't see Craig in that light!'

In spite of herself, Debbie laughed and said: 'No, I'm sure that Craig has been accused of many things in his time but never that! No, it's just that I think he took a liberty with me the other night although he says I'm making too much of what happened.'

She paused and then said shyly: 'Ivor, if I told you what the row was about, would you give me your honest opinion as to whether I'm being too fussy? I'd love to hear what another man has to say about it.'

'Well, I'm not sure about that,' said Ivor doubtfully. 'I wouldn't want to upset either you or Craig.'

'But I promise I won't tell Craig that I've spoken to you,' said Debbie quickly, 'and I'd be ever so obliged if you'd hear me out. It won't take long and Trish came in early and she doesn't mind sitting on reception whilst she has her coffee.'

Ivor looked at his watch and let out a little sigh. He had planned to plough through the latest press cuttings on his clients before starting work in earnest, but on the other hand it was important to keep the staff happy – and in any case, he was intrigued to find out what had so annoyed the pretty girl.

So he told Debbie to sit herself down and settled back to listen to her story, noting with admiration her long, shapely legs as he sipped his tea.

'It was last Tuesday evening and Craig had come round to our house after supper – I live with my Mum and Dad, you know. Well, they'd gone out to the pictures and Craig and I were in the lounge listening to some records and having a cuddle when the phone rang. It was my friend, Norma, and I knew that I was going to be there for a while because she loves to chat.

'Anyhow, a minute or so later I heard a ring on the doorbell and I called out to Craig to answer it. Whilst I was listening to Norma I heard the front door close and I saw Craig go back in the lounge with his friend Harry who he had said might pop round as Harry had two spare tickets for the Rolling Stones concert which we could buy from him.

'Now I should explain that my Dad is a cabinet maker and we keep our telephone on top of a lovely big cupboard that Dad made when he was an apprentice, and I'm in the habit of kneeling on the chair beside it, resting my elbows on the cupboard. Well, I was chatting away to Norma when all of a sudden I felt Craig's hand lifting up my skirt from behind, showing

9

off my bottom and my little bikini panties to Harry as well as himself.

'I covered the mouthpiece with my hand and hissed: "Stop it, Craig!" before continuing my conversation with Norma. He took no notice, though, and a few seconds later I could feel his hand sliding up my leg and caressing the back of my thigh. So I reached round and slapped his hand really hard, but this didn't stop him either and he started to kiss my bum through my tight white knickers.

'"Hold on a minute, Norma," I said and turned round to see Harry standing there grinning like a Cheshire cat. "Bugger off!" I whispered fiercely to Craig and turned back to speak to Norma, who was giving me a detailed description of a marvellous fuck she'd enjoyed on Sunday night with Louis, her new boyfriend, who had the thickest prick she'd ever seen in her life.

'Meanwhile, though, Craig wouldn't stop playing with my bum and with one ear I was listening to Norma and with the other ear I could hear him whispering to Harry if he would like to see how gorgeous my soft, rounded bum cheeks looked without being covered by my skimpy panties.'

Debbie paused and bit her lip. 'I do hope I'm not going to shock you now, Ivor, 'cos I wouldn't want you to think badly of me, she said as a light pink blush coloured her cheeks.'

'I can't believe I'd ever do that,' Ivor quickly assured her and with an easy smile, he added: 'and believe me, Debbie, I've got more than enough skeletons rattling in my wardrobe to prove it!'

10

She looked gratefully at him and smoothed her hand across her face before continuing: 'Thanks, Ivor, you are kind. I knew you'd be sympathetic.'

'I'll take that as a compliment,' he grinned and told her to carry on with her story.

She nodded and, moistening her lips with her tongue, she continued: 'Well now, not to beat about the bush, Craig just kept going on and on about my glorious bum and my juicy pussy, and then instead of his fingers I could feel his warm, very hard cock brushing over my panties. This made me feel very randy and I felt myself getting wet and this time I reached round and instead of smacking him, I squeezed his shaft and began giving him a slow wank whilst I listened to how Norma's boyfriend managed to bring her off three times before he spunked.

'I had trouble keeping my voice steady because Craig was pulling my panties over my arse and sliding his smooth knob between my bum cheeks. Instinctively, I pushed out my bottom and he slipped my knickers down to my knees as his shaft slithered its way into my sticky wet cunt from behind.

'"Ooooh!" I moaned as he began to fuck me in a lovely slow rhythm, pumping in and out of my tingling snatch. Thank goodness Norma kept rabbiting on as I was in no state to carry on a conversation!

'"Oh, I've got to go now, Debs, there's something I want to see on the telly. I'll ring up again tomorrow night," she said. Which was just as well because I couldn't concentrate on anything else as Craig was fucking me now with long, steady strokes which made

11

me almost swoon with pleasure. I put down the phone and then I gasped when Harry came and stood in front of me, ripping open his flies and taking out his big boner which he held in his hand just inches from my lips.

'I leaned forward and started to gobble him, laying my cheek along his hot, stiff shaft and nibbling his balls and licking up and down the barrel of his cock before sucking his knob deep inside my mouth.

'Harry whimpered with pleasure as I sucked his shaft, bobbing my head up and down his rigid rod, and my lips slurped noisily on his thick cock as the top of his helmet slid along the roof of my mouth to the back of my throat.

'Watching me suck off his friend drove Craig wild and he began to slam his cock in and out of my tight, wet cunt and when his hand came round to rub my clitty, my whole body started to shudder and I climaxed just as Craig jetted his jism into me from the rear and Harry spurted a deluge of spunk into my mouth. I swallowed as much of his salty cum as I could and I heard Craig say to Harry: "There you are, mate, didn't I tell you that Debbie's a horny girl?"'

'Ah, so you believe that the whole episode was planned and that's why you're angry with Craig,' Ivor ventured and Debbie drew her chair closer to him and laid a hand on his knee.

'I'm absolutely certain of it, Ivor,' she said firmly. 'Of course, they weren't to know that Norma was going to call me but Harry hadn't just brought round the concert tickets – he'd also come with a big bottle of Babycham as well as half a dozen cans of lager.'

'So they thought you wouldn't object so much to a threesome if you were a bit tiddley,' remarked Ivor as he crossed his legs to try and hide his own bulging erection. 'Well, I must say I'd have thought that a sophisticated chap like Craig would have had more finesse.'

Debbie brushed back a strand of silky auburn hair from her face as she said with great feeling: 'So did I! I wouldn't have minded if he'd have asked me straight out. It so happened that I've always fancied Harry and if he hadn't have pulled his cock out for me to suck, I'd have taken it out for him! And I know that they're both nice lads and neither of them would try and force me to do anything I didn't want to.'

'I don't know Craig that well,' said Ivor, although memories of a riotous orgy up in Scotland with Cable Publicity's market research director flashed across his mind. 'But it seems quite out of character. If you like, I'll have a quiet word, man-to-man, with him and perhaps we can sort it all out.'

'So you agree that I'm right to be cross with him?'

'For what it's worth, Debbie, I think you've every right to be angry with Craig. He should have sounded you out first – as one of the old Latin poets put it, *Quae dant, quaeque negant, gaudent tamen esse rogatae*.'

Debbie looked at him and giggled. 'Blimey, what does that mean?'

'Whether they give or refuse, women always want to be asked,' he translated and Debbie nodded her head and said: 'Exactly! And I'd be very grateful if you'd have a word with Craig as I'm not speaking to him till he apologises on his bended knees.'

'That sounds a bit strong,' remarked Ivor with a twinkle in his eye but Debbie replied by moving her chair even closer to him and murmuring: 'Well, I'd accept his apology and then he'd be in a perfect position to eat my pussy. He may have upset me but I must admit that I don't half miss what Craig's been doing to me in his office every morning before we start work.'

Despite Debbie's uninhibited outlook, this bold confession shocked Ivor and all he could do was to nod weakly when Debbie jumped up and said: 'I'd better lock the door whilst I tell you what we do.'

She returned and stood in front of him and then she whispered huskily: 'I always take off my knickers as soon as I get to the office. Then I go to Craig's office and he lifts up my skirt and brings me off with his tongue. Would you like to take his place this morning, Ivor? I'll bet you're a great pussy-eater.'

Ivor gulped and ran his hand round the inside of the collar of his shirt as Debbie pulled up her skirt to reveal the cluster of auburn curls between her thighs. He breathed deeply when, with slow deliberation, the nubile young girl traced the outline of her slit with her forefinger and then cradled the back of his head in her hands.

He made no attempt to resist as she pulled his head forward and he kissed her moist love-crack, pressing his lips on her pussy and running his tongue up and down the long slit, which made her thighs tremble as Debbie squeaked happily with delight.

'Oooh, Ivor! Oooh, Oooh, that's gorgeous!' she groaned with sensual fervour, grinding her hips from side to side whilst Ivor inhaled the pungent aroma of her moistening pussy.

For a brief moment Ivor drew back and then he slid out of his chair and down upon the rich, wine-coloured rug and he plunged his head back between Debbie's thighs, burrowing his face deep inside her welcoming quim.

'Yes, yes, yes!' she panted as Ivor's hands clasped the soft cushions of her buttocks whilst he teased her clitty with the tip of his tongue, opening her love lips and licking up the pungent love juice which was already beginning to flow through her pink cunny lips which were glistening with evident excitement.

Debbie's body quivered all over with lustful pleasure and her shudderings increased in intensity until she stepped back and dropped down on her knees to plant a passionate, open-mouthed kiss on Ivor's lips which neither of them seemed keen to end. Then she thrust back her head and moaned: 'Oh, fuck me, Ivor, please fuck me!'

It took only seconds for Ivor to unbuckle his belt and pull down his trousers and boxer shorts whilst Debbie wiggled out of her skirt. She lay back and in a flash he was on top of her and his pulsating, erect shaft was slicking its way in and out of her juicy honeypot.

A sudden thought crossed his mind and he began: 'Debbie, are you – ' but she correctly guessed his question and she gasped wildly: 'Don't worry, I'm on the Pill! Go on, Ivor, stuff that stiff pole right

15

up me! Oh, that's the way, fill me with cock, I love it!'

Ivor gritted his teeth and he drove deep inside the luscious love channel, their bodies thrashing around back and forth as they gloried in their wild and wanton love-making. Debbie crossed her legs over his back and he pressed his lips against hers as they clung madly to each other whilst he frantically jabbed his shaft in and out of her sopping slit. Ivor grunted with ecstasy as her cunt squeezed his throbbing prick with vice-like muscles and, when he felt himself approaching his orgasm, he slid his hand under her backside and sank a finger between her bum cheeks which took Debbie over the top.

From the back of her throat came a hoarse cry of satisfaction as her body arched upwards to take in the last thrust of Ivor's twitching tool, and as the sticky, whitish seed burst out of his pulsating prick, Debbie climaxed in great, all-over shudders, bouncing up and down underneath Ivor's body, her hair flying from side to side as he pumped further thick gushes of warm cum inside her sopping crack, splashing against the outer folds of her pussy and dribbling down her thighs to mingle with her own love juices which had gushed out of her saturated cunt.

They lay in an exhausted heap of entwined limbs for a couple of minutes until they were startled into frantic activity by a knock on the door.

'Ivor, are you in there?' exclaimed a soft female voice and as he scrambled to his feet Ivor called back to his secretary: 'Morning, Suzie, I'm tied-up in a private meeting just now. Go to your office and I'll be with you in about five minutes.'

He stepped into his pants and Debbie slipped on her skirt and wriggled her feet back into her shoes. 'Bloody hell, do you think she's guessed what we've been up to?' asked Ivor anxiously as he pulled up his trousers.

'It's possible, but I wouldn't worry about it,' said Debbie cheerfully. 'Suzie's a sweet girl and she won't spread any gossip about us. Look, it's no big deal – after all, she told me only a few days after I joined Cable Publicity that most of the girls here end up being fucked by you, Martin or one of the other directors.'

Ivor blushed as he buttoned up his shirt and he muttered: 'God, if that's the kind of a reputation we've built up, we'll need to employ a public relations agency for Cable Publicity!'

Debbie giggled at his embarrassment and put her finger to his lips. 'Don't fret, Ivor, I'm sure there have never been any bad vibes about it as far as any of the girls have been concerned. This is a fun place to work in, lots of nice people and, although we sometimes have to put in crazy hours when we're busy, the pay's quite generous.'

'I'm glad to hear you say that,' said Ivor with some interest. 'Between you and me, I'm the one who pushed through the idea of a summer bonus and an annual pay rise. You get that extra commitment from a happy staff.'

'Thats right; agreed Debbie 'and it's not as if any girl here has ever been told that she must let her boss have her or she'll never be promoted. I mean, everyone knows that in his department Mr Horne's been screwing Judy Jones but he appointed Roberta to be his personal assistant last month, although of course she doesn't put out for any of the men.'

Ivor gave a faint smile and said: 'I'm glad to hear you say that, Debbie, because I don't approve of sexual blackmail. It's neither a moral nor an efficient way to run a business.'

She kissed his cheek and picked up his mug of tea. 'I'll wash this up and leave it on Suzie's desk,' she said as she walked towards the door. 'Do let me know what Craig says when you've had words with him.'

'I will,' Ivor promised as he settled down into his chair and picked up an envelope marked 'Private and Confidential' which must have been placed on his desk after he had left the office the previous evening. 'And be a pal, ask Suzie to come in here as soon as she has a minute.'

'Will do,' she said as she blew him a farewell kiss, unlocked the door and swept out into the corridor.

Ivor stretched out his arms and then permitted himself a short chuckle as he idly thought about bringing up for discussion at the next board meeting a plan to ensure that all directors began the day with a thumping good fuck. It would do us all a power of good and set ourselves up nicely for a hard day's work, he could argue, and as there appeared to be a plethora of willing girls in the office who would be happy to oblige, the proposal wouldn't cost anything and might do wonders for staff morale!

Ah well, back to reality, he murmured quietly as he

opened the envelope which contained a memorandum from Martin Reese which read:

Ivor, I want you and Craig Grey to meet a Mr Keith Seed and his business partner, an Israeli guy named Bennie Hynek, at noon today. If necessary, cancel any appointments already in your diary because these two chaps could put a nice little earner our way.

Briefly, they have secured UK and European rights to market an amazing new cream this Israeli guy has manufactured using a special compound of salts from the Dead Sea which, if you rub it on your John Thomas, will make and keep it as stiff as a poker till your partner begs you to shoot your load.

The cream is one hundred per cent safe to use and is so effective that Keith Seed says he's prepared to offer a 'money back if not satisfied' guarantee with every jar of cream sold.

If the product is as good as he claims, then I'm so sure he'll make a fortune that if Keith Seed wanted any development capital to begin selling this cream, I'd open my cheque book like a shot in exchange for a small part of the action. However, he doesn't need financing as he's a wealthy chap in his own right, being a director of his family firm which owns a chain of twenty chemists' shops in the Home Counties.

He'll sell the stuff through his own shops, of course, but to begin with, he plans to test the market via a mail-order operation before taking the plunge and hiring a sales team to sell to other chemists and druggists.

Naturally, Keith needs a first class publicity campaign to promote the cream (for starters, we need a good name for it) and you might not believe it, Ivor, but it was none other than your old friend George Lucas of Tagholm and Thomson who recommended us to him!

Phone me at eleven o'clock this morning on Hampstead 2305 and we'll discuss this further.

Ivor laid down the sheet of paper and whistled softly as he contemplated the contents of Martin's note. If this cream could really deliver the goods and prolong a man's control over his cock, then as his boss had written, this stuff would sell like hot cakes. He knew of at least one friend who had confided to Ivor that he suffered from the dreaded 'hair-trigger' syndrome and was prone to ejaculate as soon as he began fucking, and Mandy Harcourt, Ivor's girlfriend who was a copywriter in a small, hotshot advertising agency, had told him that her sister's current boyfriend also suffered from the same complaint.

'Sheila says that poor Tom's cock stiffens up without any trouble but she only has to touch it and often he can't stop himself spunking before he's even slipped it into her pussy,' Mandy had remarked only last Sunday morning whilst she and Ivor were snuggled up in bed together after enjoying a marathon all-night session of love-making.

This product could prove to be a real boom, Ivor decided, as he reached for his diary. Fortunately the only entries for the day were a lunch-date with an old friend from his college days and a meeting about his new company car with Garry Horne, the agency's finance director, which could both be easily rearranged without any problem.

'Come in,' he called out in answer to a loud knock on his door, and he glanced up to smile at his secretary who came in bearing a tray piled high with the morning mail.

'Hiya, Suzie, sorry about keeping you waiting just before,' he mumbled uncomfortably, but the stunning raven-haired girl simply smiled as she drew up a chair and sat down, crossing her long, shapely legs in a manner which never failed to excite her boss. 'I just had to get some private business out of the way before getting down to work.'

'Oh, no problem, Ivor, though I thought you had already got down to an early start with Debbie from reception,' said Suzie airily as she picked up her notepad and a biro from the mail tray.

Wisely, Ivor decided not to take the bait and carried on hurriedly, saying: 'Is there anything in the post which requires immediate attention? No? Good, then just send out the usual I'll-be-in-touch-soon holding letters where necessary whilst I make a couple of check calls about Ruff Trayde. But first I'd like you to read through this note from Martin, which I'd like to talk over with you in about half an hour. Then please cancel my lunch date with Fred Nolan. Give him my apologies and tell him I'll call him tomorrow, and you'd better buzz Garry Horne and ask him if I can postpone our chat till later this afternoon or first thing tomorrow morning.'

He handed Martin's memo to his secretary and as usual, despite the fact that he had only just recovered from an exhilarating fuck, Ivor felt a familiar stirring in his groin as Suzie leaned forward to take the paper from him. As usual, the top two buttons of her white blouse were undone and he was given a superb view of the cleavage between her generous breasts.

'Okay, I'll come back in at a quarter past ten. If anyone telephones, shall I say you're in a meeting, or is there anyone you want to speak to?'

'Hold all my calls, but put anyone through if you think I should speak to them,' said Ivor, who was content to leave this important task to Suzie's uncannily accurate judgement in such matters.

After Suzie had left the office he tried hard to concentrate on the Ruff Trayde file. Ruff's new single, *When Will The Telephone Ring?* had shot into the hit parade but had only reached the number five position despite two appearances on *Top Of The Pops* and was in urgent need of a 'hype' just to hold its place, because the previous week The Animals, Cilla Black and Herman's Hermits had all released new records which would shoot up the charts very quickly. Ivor gnawed at his bottom lip as he contemplated the problem – Cable Publicity's contract with Ruff's management ended in less than a month and although the fees were relatively small, no agency liked losing an account and the appearance of a high-profile showbiz account on their list of clients had helped to attract a sizeable amount of new business.

Cable had gained the account because Bob Mackswell, the impressario who owned Ruff and a stable of other young pop stars, had been a great friend of Martin Reese whilst they were studying at Oxford University. Although other publicity agencies were continually offering their services to his expanding organisation, Mackswell had so far brushed them aside and Cable's position had been further strengthened when Ivor's former secretary, Sheena Shackleton, had accepted a job as Mackswell's personal assistant. However, if Ruff's new record failed to reach the top spot (which looked increasingly likely), there was bound to be an inquest and in Ivor's experience, at such post-mortems it was always agreed by the production and sales teams that the major factor for any failure was the lack of good publicity! He didn't altogether blame the people in a company who often unfairly pointed the finger at an outside supplier such as the publicity agency when things went wrong. These days all the executives were busy covering their arses with the economy in deepening disarray, with unemployment creeping up to the half million mark and financial pundits threatening a devaluation of the pound.

Ivor sighed heavily as he picked up the telephone and dialled Sheena Shackleton's private line at the Mackswell Organisation. 'Hi there, how's the cleverest, prettiest, sexiest, most adorable girl in London?' he asked.

'Suspicious,' replied Sheena, who might not have won any contests for such Olympian attributes but was nonetheless a bright, extremely attractive girl in her early twenties whose light blue eyes were always wide-open and attentive and who usually wore her long blonde hair tied back in a pony tail with a straight fringe brushed down onto her forehead. Ivor had lusted after his secretary, especially when he had chanced to see a set of sensual colour photographs of her taken by a boyfriend which she had accidently left on top of her desk. Several shots showed Sheena in the nude except for a pair of minute bikini panties, and the memory of her creamy white, jutting breasts and her big brown nipples had haunted him for weeks, but she had made it quite clear to Ivor that she was spoken for, a position which he had naturally if regretfully accepted, though they had stayed on good terms during the seven months they worked together.

'As you should be, my love. You're absolutely right not to be taken in by any handsome, sophisticated publicist who only calls when he wants some information from you,' he said smoothly, leaning back in his chair and swivelling it round to face the window.

'Thanks for the advice, Ivor, if anyone like that ever rings me, I won't listen to a word of what he has to say,' she replied crisply.

Ivor chuckled and went on: 'So, how's Bob taking to the fact that Ruff's new release is probably on the slide? I suppose that we've been slagged off because Maureen Cleave decided that she didn't want to interview Ruff for the *Standard*.'

'Well, you're hardly the flavour of the month but then no-one else is, either,' said Sheena and lowering her voice she added: 'between you and me, Ivor, in my opinion the song's just not strong enough. Tony Mulliken and Steve Williams both begged Bob to

24

make *When Will The Telephone Ring*? a B side and commission a top team like Bernie Rubin and Tony Hammond to write something for Ruff, but you know the score . . .'

'Indeed I do,' said Ivor heavily, for he was aware that *When Will The Telephone Ring*? had been composed by one of Ruff's secret boyfriends who fancied himself as a songwriter and that to keep his biggest star happy, Bob Mackswell had uncharacteristically agreed to Ruff's demand to release the song as his next single. 'And to be honest, I don't think we can do more than a damage limitation exercise at this stage. Look, any chance of a meet later today?'

'Yes, I think we have to show Bob that we've some fresh ideas to try and keep the record in the charts. Can you come round at about half past five? Bob and Ruff are in Brighton but Tony Mulliken will be here and we can put our heads together and plan out a new campaign.'

'Okay, darling, I'll see you later. *Ciao*,' said Ivor but when he replaced the receiver he suddenly remembered that he had promised to take his girlfriend Mandy out to the cinema tonight. I'd better call her and change the arrangements, he muttered as he dialled her company's number.

'Osbourne and Webb Associates, may I help you?' said the operator after only two rings, and Ivor made a mental note to mention the need for a second receptionist/telephonist to Martin Reese, because sometimes one had to wait ages to get through to Cable when Debbie's switchboard was overloaded and this not only irritated callers but gave an undeserved, inefficient image to the agency. 'Amanda Harcourt, please,' he asked and he smiled when his girlfriend picked up the phone.

He cleared his throat and said: 'Mandy, hi, it's me, how's it going? Look, I'm very sorry but a slight problem's come up about tonight.'

'Ivor, you're not going to let me down, are you? I'm dying to see *The Wrong Box*,' she said reproachfully.

'So am I, love, and that's still on, don't worry. Thanks to our Mackswell connection, I've booked tickets so we won't have to queue. The only thing is that I know you prefer to eat before we go out, but I've got to go to a meeting in Chelsea this afternoon and I doubt if I'll be able to get away much before seven o'clock.'

'Oh, is that all?' said Mandy with relief. 'Well, that's no big deal, darling. It so happens that I've also got a rush job on and wouldn't mind putting in a little overtime tonight. Pick me up at the office at half past seven, or a bit earlier if possible. You can come back to my place afterwards and I'll rustle up an omelette and a nice salad.'

'Sounds good to me,' said Ivor and he beamed happily when Mandy added softly: 'And my new flat-mate, Jilly, is out of town and won't be back till tomorrow night.'

This would be an unexpected pleasure and he blew a kiss down the line and said happily: 'Better and better, I'll be round as near half past seven as possible. Bye for now, love.'

He only had time to contemplate the joys of staying the night with Mandy for a minute or two before Suzie popped her head through the door. 'Ivor, Martin tele-phoned a couple of minutes ago but you were engaged. Would you ring him back immediately at the number he gave you?'

'Okay, Suzie, I'll call him back this very minute,' he replied and dialled the digits which he knew would connect him to the home of Martin's stunning young West Indian personal assistant. Sure enough a sensual female voice answered the phone and Ivor said: 'Carole, is that you? Hi there, it's Ivor here. I'm returning Martin's call.'

'Hello, Ivor, hold on a moment and I'll bring the phone to him,' said Carole coolly without a hint of embarrassment in her voice.

Surely you mean you'll bring him to the phone, thought Ivor idly as he waited for his boss. 'Hiya, Ivor, how are you?' said Martin chirpily. 'Have you read my note about Keith Seed and Bennie Hynek? What do you think about this fantastic new stay-hard cream? I reckon it could be a real winner.'

'If it works,' said Ivor carefully, but Martin waved aside his caution and said: 'You ask Carole about it. I rubbed some on my prick last night and we've been banging all night, haven't we, honey? Oh Christ, don't do that, you horny girl, how the hell can I carry on an intelligent conversation whilst you're sucking me off?'

Ivor licked his lips as in his mind's eye he saw the nude, full-breasted figure of Carole kneeling beside Martin with her hand wrapped around his throbbing erection and her pink tongue delicately licking the sensitive underside of his shaft. He pulled at the front of his trousers to allow his own swelling cock to rise up and form a huge bulge in his lap as he heard Martin groan: 'For heaven's sake, Carole, stop gobbling my cock, I'm trying to talk to Ivor,' but he didn't sound as if he really meant it.

'Okay, you win, love. Sorry, Ivor old boy, Carole's going down on me and I can't speak any more. Bloody hell, she's wanking me off with her hand whilst she's licking my balls. Got to go before I come, if you understand me! Best of luck with the meeting. You'll like Keith and Bennie – take them to Aldo's in Charlotte Street for lunch and I'll meet you there for coffee at about two o'clock.'

Martin rang off and Ivor sat there transfixed for a few moments and then he breathed deeply and called up Craig Grey on the internal phone. 'Good morning, Craig, how are you? Tell me, did Martin copy you in on his note to me about this prospective new client he wants us to take out for lunch today? Yes? Then could you please come down to my office for a chat at half past eleven? Super, see you soon.'

Suzie now reappeared and shut the door behind her. 'I've dealt with the post. It was all pretty routine stuff which can wait till this afternoon,' she announced as she walked across and sat down in front of his desk. 'Now then, you said you wanted to talk about this note from Martin about this magic cream which can transform a man's performance between the sheets. If it works, Martin's mates could make a fortune.'

'That's what Martin believes,' he remarked, strumming the fingers of his right hand on the top of his desk diary. 'I'm not too sure how much of a need there is for the product, although I must say that I can think of two chaps who might be interested in it.'

'Well, I can think of a third,' said Suzie promptly. 'The guy I met at a party last Saturday night could have used it, that's for sure.'

Ivor sat up straight and said in a shocked voice: 'Suzie! I'm surprised at you – I thought you and that guy Jeffrey what's-his-name who's a features writer on the *Observer* were an item.'

'So did I,' she replied, tossing back an offending strand of silky, long dark hair from her face. 'But you remember we worked late on Friday evening mapping out the campaign for Sid Cohen's Antiques Fair in Islington?'

'Yes, of course, it was good of you to stay on. No-one likes doing any overtime on a Friday night. God, I hope I wasn't the cause of your falling out with Jeff.'

'In no way, Ivor,' she said firmly. 'In fact you did me a real favour. I didn't mind working late that much and you did take me out for a lovely dinner afterwards! And, as I say, if it hadn't been for you I might never have found out that Jeff Hammersmith is a lying little toe-rag who I never want to clap eyes on again!'

'Strong words, Suzie, you're sure you aren't just in the middle of a little lovers' tiff?' he murmured, but she shook her head fiercely and said: 'I won't stand for being two-timed, Ivor, and that's exactly what Jeff was doing behind my back.

'Do you remember that when we left the restaurant on Friday night I told you how I was going on to see Jeff when you offered me a lift home? Actually, although I'd told him that I would phone if I didn't finish work too late, I didn't bother to call because I thought I'd give him a nice surprise by turning up at his pad and staying the night with him. Now, by mistake Jeff had left a set of keys to his place in my flat and I thought this would give me an ideal opportunity to return them.

'So I took a taxi to his flat and once inside the house I opened the front door and gently closed it behind me. At first I thought Jeff had gone out to the cinema or to the pub because all the lights were off and I couldn't hear the radio or television. But then I heard some muffled laughter coming from Jeff's bedroom and I tip-toed down the hall and round the corner to see just what was going on. He'd left the bedroom door open and his bedside light was on so I had a grandstand view of my dear boyfriend and a sumptuous young girl with enormous big knockers lying naked together on his bed. I saw him lean over and suck one of her long pink nips into his mouth and she giggled and said: "You can't leave my titties alone, can you, you naughty boy?"

'"Oh yes I can," Jeff replied and as he slipped his finger into her fluffy dark muff she spread her legs to allow him to finger-fuck her. She wriggled like mad when Jeff slid two more fingers into her cunt and I must admit that I began to feel randy myself as I watched her take hold of his thick stiffie in her hand and start tossing him off.

'Jeff twisted round and kissed her nipples which made her start moaning: "Oh, lovely, lovely . . . that's it, use your tongue on my tits, circle it round quickly, oooh, you're making them so hard!"

'Then she let go of his tadger and I heard her whisper: "Come on, Jeff, fuck my cunny with your fat cock, you rascal!"

'He raised himself on top of her and she wrapped her legs around him as he guided his shaft inside her. I stood there silently, watching his arse heaving up and down as he pumped his prick in and out of her squelchy love channel, and I wondered how he'd feel if I suddenly walked in and snapped on the bedroom light.'

She paused and Ivor gave her a lop-sided little smile. 'And did you?' he enquired, but Suzie slowly shook her head and said: 'No, I soon decided just to quietly walk back to the front door and once I was outside I dropped Jeff's keys through the letter box. That would be a more dignified way to let him know that the game was up. And also, if I'd have made a scene, it wouldn't have been very fair on the girl, who I'd never seen before and who probably didn't even suspect that Jeff was supposed to be *my* boyfriend, though I suppose if I had have interrupted them and given Jeff a piece of my mind, she would have known the kind of double-crossing rat she had between her thighs!'

'I agree with you,' said Ivor as he leaned forward and gave her arm a comforting little squeeze. 'And I can just imagine what Jeff's reaction would have been if he had found you in bed with another man!'

'Quite so, though that's now only a hypothetical situation,' declared Suzie warmly. 'I'm now a free agent and I'm not really into spectator sports in the bedroom like some girls I know round here.'

Ivor pricked up his ears at this fascinating news –

who the devil could Suzie be talking about? But he decided to try and winkle out this information at a more suitable time and simply said: 'So last Saturday night you decided to demonstrate to Jeff that what's sauce for the goose is sauce for the gander?'

Suzie shrugged her shoulders and replied: 'Perhaps there was an element of tit for tat in my behaviour, because I promise you, Ivor, I'm not in the habit of jumping into bed with every Tom, Dick and Harry I meet.'

'Certainly not with any old Dick,' agreed Ivor solemnly, which made Suzie giggle despite herself. 'Well, as it happens the boy who spent Saturday night with me was a Dick! Dickie Ressler as a matter of fact. You might have bumped into him, come to think of it, as Dickie's the media buyer at Osbourne and Webb Associates, the agency where your girlfriend works.'

'Y-e-s-s, I seem to remember Mandy introducing me to him a few weeks ago,' said Ivor thoughtfully. 'A smartly dressed chap of about my age, on the stocky side, dark hair and a ruddy complexion. Seemed a very nice chap to me though we only chatted for a few minutes.'

'He *is* a nice chap, Ivor. I met him at this party which Estelle, a girlfriend of mine, threw last Saturday night and we hit it off from the moment we met. He's a jolly, amusing man and when after a while I told Dickie about how I'd been badly treated and he clicked his fingers and said: "I know just what will cheer you up, Suzie, let's say bye bye to Estelle and go and catch the late show at The Establishment."

'The satirical cabaret club in Greek Street?' queried Ivor and Suzie nodded and said: 'Yup, and that's just what we did. We had a great time and afterwards when he dropped me outside my flat, I asked him to come in and have a night-cap. I asked Dickie to put on a record whilst I made the coffee and I just knew he'd choose one of my favourites. Sure enough, he'd picked out the Schubert D Minor Quartet and when I came back from the kitchen, we sat snuggled up together on the sofa listening to the lovely music whilst we drank our coffee.

'We both knew what was going to happen when he put down his mug and put his arms round me and kissed me hard on the lips. I responded by sliding my tongue inside his mouth and he did the same to me and our hands roamed all over each other's bodies as we rolled from side to side in a frenzy of passion. A feeling of intense excitement swept over me and I knew it was inevitable that I was going to be fucked by this wonderful new man.

'"Let's go to bed," I whispered in his ear and he mumured: "Yes, oh, yes, darling," as he picked me up and carried me bodily into my bedroom and deposited me gently upon the eiderdown. I kicked off my shoes and pulled off my sweater and skirt so that I lay there wearing only my bra and knickers.

'Dickie threw off all his clothes except for his underpants, through which I could see the outline of his bulging cock. He lay himself down next to me and we exchanged another luscious kiss as he unhooked my bra and I lifted my bum so that he could pull down my panties. Then I tugged down his pants and the sight of his thick, circumcised prick made me feel as randy as hell.

'I dampened my pussy by sucking my fingers and then transferring my hand to between my legs, sliding my wet fingers all along the edges of my crack before taking Dickie's throbbing shaft in my hand and planting a moist kiss on top of his knob. He was really well-hung with at least nine inches of hard, solid meat and I was dying to feel it slide into my eager cunt.

'Dickie raised himself up over me and guided his rigid rod between my cunny lips and began to fuck me in long, sweeping strokes. Oh, God, I was in heaven, but then only after about thirty seconds came the big let-down . . .'

Ivor had quite forgotten what had triggered off Suzie's confession and now he gaped at her with a puzzled expression on his face. 'Let-down? What let-down?' he asked.

'He came before I'd even begun to start, you ninny!' answered Suzie impatiently. 'Don't you remember, when you mentioned that you were meeting these guys who are going to sell a magic new stay-hard cream, I said that I'd just met someone who needs to use it.'

Ivor smacked his forehead and grimaced. 'Sorry about that,' he apologised profusely. 'I was so engrossed by your story that everything else went out of my mind. What happened then? Perhaps Dickie was just over-excited. I don't want to embarrass you, Suzie, but you're a gorgeous girl and he was so aroused that he couldn't stop himself going over the top so quickly. I hope you don't mind my asking, but didn't you have another go?'

'Of course we did,' she replied with spirit. 'He was terribly apologetic but I kept telling him not to worry and squeezing his limp shaft in my fist, I said: "Have no fear, Dickie, I'll soon make your nice thick love truncheon strong and hard again and then we'll start all over again."'

'And did you succeed?' Ivor enquired whilst he crossed his legs in an attempt to hide his own burgeoning erection.

'Oh, I rubbed him up until his cock was standing to attention as stiff as a poker,' sighed Suzie. 'And whenever I felt he might be in danger of coming I used a technique to stop him spunking which a medical student I know told me about. I squeezed the end of his shaft just under the ridge with my thumb and two fingers and this cooled him off and his cock slowly deflated.

'Then I sucked under his helmet and that sent his tool shooting up again and when I thought he was ready to make love, I made him lie on his back and I squatted over him, sliding right down on his pulsating pole and it felt so sexy as he filled my cunt completely. I bounced up and down and I shook all over as little orgasmic sparks crackled through my entire body. However, when Dickie gasped out: "I'm coming, I'm coming!" I raised myself off his tadger for a minute and when I plunged back on it, I moved gently at first before quickening to a more enjoyable pace as I slid up and down his cock.'

Ivor smiled at her and commented: 'So all was well in the end.'

'Not really, to be honest with you,' she said with resignation. 'Dickie still spurted before I was ready, although he finished me off nicely with his fingers. The fact of the matter is that he does shoot his load too quickly for most girls and this plays on his mind so much that it makes him come even sooner! It's a kind of problem which feeds on itself.'

Ivor nodded his head in agreement. 'Yes, I can see that – every time he makes love he worries about his performance, and the more he worries, the worse he gets! Well, Suzie, we'll have to see if our new friends can help poor Dickie out. Meanwhile, I'd like you to take the minutes of the meeting with Mr Seed and Mr Hynek.'

Then he looked at her mischievously and said: 'Er, Suzie, you said something earlier on about some of the girls here liking to take part in bedroom fun and games. Who were you talking about? Scout's honour, if you tell me, I won't pass on the names to anyone else.'

She frowned and said: 'Oh no, Ivor, it wouldn't be fair. I shouldn't even have mentioned anything in the first place.'

'Oh go on, be a pal and satisfy my curiosity. I swear it will go no further,' he prompted with an engaging grin. 'Perhaps I can guess who might be involved. Mind, I'll probably be wildly wrong.'

Despite her misgivings, Suzie said drily: 'I'm not so sure you would be, Ivor. If you must know, young

Debbie in reception's top of the list. Sorry, I couldn't resist telling you that!'

She stood up and wagged a warning finger at him as he sat digesting this interesting piece of news. 'Now, don't badger me any more, Ivor, because I won't say another word about it! I'll be in my office doing some filing and I'll let you know when our visitors arrive.'

Suzie walked to the door and almost bumped into Craig Grey who stood aside to let her pass. 'Come in, Craig,' called Ivor as he mused over what Suzie had just told him. If what she said was true, it explained why Debbie had not been bothered by having a three-way sex session with Craig and his friend, Harry. As Debbie had intimated to him, if, before they had started, Cable's good-looking market research chief had asked her permission for Harry to join in the proceedings, she would not have been so angry about the whole business.

'Take a seat, mate,' said Ivor absently, as now he wondered whether he should still speak to Craig about his relationship with Debbie. I'd better have a few words with him, he decided, or Debbie will just get more and more angry and there could be a big bust-up which could mean that Cable would lose a steady, hard-working receptionist, so he reluctantly heaved himself to his feet and strode over to the window to give himself some extra time to collect his thoughts.

'Right then, I suppose you'd like some data on the sex aids market,' said Craig, as he pulled out a sheaf of papers from a large green folder.

Ivor gazed at him and said: 'Yes, in a minute, Craig,

but first I want to have a confidential word with you about a rather delicate personal matter concerning another member of our staff.'

'This must be about Debbie,' said Craig instantly and Ivor gave an awkward little nod as he walked back and slumped into his chair. 'Go on then, what's she been saying to you?'

'Look, I don't make it a practice of getting involved in people's love lives, but I'm sure you understand that if an affair starts affecting the smooth working of the office then I'm afraid I have to sort things out.'

Craig Grey was not entirely mollified by this little homily and said with a shrug: 'Fair enough, Ivor, but with respect I really don't know why you should think that my tiff with Debbie comes into that category.'

'Then I'll tell you,' said Ivor who was devoutly wishing that he hadn't opened this particular can of worms. He repeated the story which Debbie had recounted to him earlier on and he stressed how very upset she had been that Craig had introduced an uninvited guest into their love-making.

'So there we are,' finished Ivor unhappily. 'As far as I'm concerned I'm not making any judgements, and I'm not taking sides except to say that if you felt able to apologise to Debbie, I believe we could nip all this in the bud.

'Listen, I hate bad feeling in the office. It can spread into a feud, not only between those concerned but between their supporters as well as other people join in and take sides in the quarrel. You must remember how Garry Horne's secretary and that girl Sandra who used to work in your department had a blazing row and in the end they both left us?' Ivor paused and waited for any response from the other man, who was gazing down at the floor. There was silence for a few seconds before Craig lifted his head and said: 'All right, Ivor, I'll see what I can do to make it up with her.'

'Good chap,' said Ivor with genuine relief. 'I'm sure you're doing the right thing, I really am.'

'Well, I hope so, but I'll only eat humble pie if you'll listen to my side of the story, for it's obvious from what you've heard I come out of this business very badly. No, no, Ivor, don't attempt to deny it, you must think that I've been a right pig.'

Ivor protested weakly that he thought nothing of the kind, but Craig stuck to his guns and in the end he was forced to capitulate and he sank back in his chair to hear what Craig had to say.

Cable's research chief put down his papers on Ivor's desk and began: 'I'll make no bones about it, I freely admit that as soon as I met Debbie I fancied her something rotten and I tried to date her only a few days after she started working here.

'And I wasn't the only one, was I, Ivor? Christ, I wouldn't be surprised if you and Martin have already fucked her because I'm no longer fooled by those big, wide eyes and the soulful pout of her lips! Believe me, Ivor, underneath that little-girl-lost look there's a real raver lurking!'

This put Ivor in a bit of a spot but before he was about to fib and deny any sexual shenanigans with Debbie, Craig held up his hand and stopped him, saying: 'No, don't tell me, I don't want to know – one way or the other, it doesn't matter, Debbie and I have always been very open-minded about either of us having other partners if we wanted to play away occasionally. So I wouldn't be angry with you, but it's not really an issue here. Let me tell you a little more about my first encounter with her.

'She had come up to my office one lunchtime with a telephone message she'd taken for me whilst I'd been at a meeting, and I chatted her up and shared my sandwiches with her. She was wearing a bright green miniskirt and a cream cotton blouse without a bra, which meant that I could see the outline of her round breasts quite clearly under the thin, semi-transparent material, and they jiggled so sexily when she moved around my office.

'So when she asked me where she could find Graham Bowe's office, I made an excuse to her that I also wanted a word with Graham to give me the opportunity of escorting her there myself. I opened the door to let her leave my office in front of me, and when Debbie climbed the stairs up to the next floor I was certain that she deliberately wiggled her bum to give me a cock-wrenching flash of her panties.

'I found something to ask Graham and waited for Debbie to leave some prints which had been left at the reception desk for him. On the way back to my office I asked her if she would like to have a quick bite after work that evening and then go on to Ronnie Scott's jazz club to hear Julian Clayton's new big band. She said she'd love to and we had a terrific time together.

'I drove her home and Debbie asked me in for coffee. She said to me with a saucy look that she was all alone that week because her parents were away in Majorca, and so she would be relieved to have a man around the house during the night.'

'You must have thought that Christmas had come early,' Ivor remarked and Craig grunted: 'Yes, something like that, I suppose. Blow me down, Ivor, sure enough, after the coffee we made inroads into a bottle of white wine and before you could say Jack Robinson, we were rolling about in Debbie's bed and tearing off each other's clothes. My hands were roving everywhere, feeling her tits and clutching her peachy bum cheeks as she pressed herself against me.

'When she was naked she lay back, stretched out her legs and started to tweak her titties till they stood out like hard brown corks whilst I gazed on her fluffy tuft of dark pussy hair between her thighs. She pulled down my pants and grasped hold of my cock. "Let me do some of the work, Craig," she whispered as she clambered up and straddled my huge, raging hard-on.

'She twiddled her fingers round her cunny lips and settled herself on my helmet before sinking down on my cock. She began to slide up and down on my cock with a blissful smile on her face, driving up and down so quickly that I felt my embedded prick belonged to her just as much as it did to me! I rubbed my palms against her stalky nipples as she slicked her cunt faster and faster on my twitching tool, gyrating her hips whilst I grabbed hold of her gorgeous buttocks and jerked my body upwards in time to meet her downward thrusts.

Watching her luscious body slide up and down my shaft was exciting enough in itself, but the sensations of her cunny muscles nipping my prick were so strong that I soon drenched the walls of her cunt and Debbie screamed and thrust her body on top of me, rubbing her nipples against my chest as she, too, exploded into a tremendous orgasm.'

Craig mopped his brow and let out a deep breath. 'Ivor, since then, I've fucked Debbie anywhere and everywhere in every possible way. But it was only shortly after this first fuck that Debbie started dropping hints about how much fun it would be if we invited another person to come to bed with us. Well, early one morning in my office, she brought up the subject again and I told her that I'd never even imagined taking part in a threesome. Now truthfully, I believed Debbie was talking about bringing in another girl to join in our love-making, so when she finally asked me if I were game to give it a whirl, I said that I'd love to!

'"Great, come round to my friend Frankie's house tonight at about ten, and we'll have a groovy time," she said delightedly and I said that the very idea made me feel very sexy.

'"Super! But don't even *think* about having a wank today," she warned me, giving my cock a friendly squeeze as she slipped past me to go back to the reception desk. "No danger, darling, I need to keep all my strength for tonight," I called after her, though funnily enough, later that afternoon I was given a come-on by one of Garry Horne's girls in accounts.'

'Not Rosie with the huge knockers who left after

the office party last Christmas?' asked Ivor with a chuckle, and Craig nodded before he went on: 'I'm not surprised, she was a very naughty lady indeed – did you know that she seduced young Philip, Garry's sixteen-year-old nephew, who'd been helping Tom in the post-room during the pre-Christmas rush? Martin thought that she'd done the lad a favour by taking his cherry, but Garry wasn't pleased at all as he'd also been knocking her off, so we gave Rosie her cards. Last I heard she was working as a hostess at the Astor Club making a fortune out of the Arabs!

'Carry on, though, Craig, I shouldn't have interrupted you,' he finished.

'That's okay, Ivor, there's not much more to tell. Debbie gave me the address of her friend and I could hardly wait to see what this second girl would be like – would she be slim or plump, a blonde or a brunette? Anyway, at ten o'clock on the dot I walked up the drive and rang the bell. I waited for about half a minute but there was no answer, so I rang again and this time, after only a few seconds, Debbie herself came to the door.

'"Hello, Craig, my word, you're punctual!' she said, giving me a saucy wink as she ushered me in. 'Can't wait to try out something new, h'm? Well, you're in luck, I also arrived early so come into the lounge and meet Frankie. We'll have a drink and that'll let you two get to know each other before we move into the bedroom."

'I eagerly followed her through the hallway, not suspecting for a moment what a tremendous shock was in store for me in the lounge!

'"Craig, I'd like you to meet Frankie Macdougall," she said sweetly and who should rise up from the sofa but a slim, soft-featured young guy of no more than eighteen, dressed in a black leather jacket and jeans!

'"Hiya, Craig, how's it going?" he said easily as he held out his hand.

'"Not too bad, thanks," I replied weakly as we shook hands, and Debbie pushed a glass of red wine between my fingers. I sat down rather heavily in an armchair and said: "Listen, you must forgive me if I look a bit surprised, but when Debbie mentioned something about Frankie, I automatically assumed she was talking about a girlfriend!"

'He grinned and said: "Sorry to disappoint you – but you're not the first to make that mistake." He turned to Debbie and wagged a reproving finger at her. "Debs, I told you before to make things clear to Craig. You're a naughty girl and you really deserve to have your bum smacked."

'"Promises, promises," Debbie said teasingly and in a flash she lifted her skirt and tugged down her knickers. Then she stepped out of them, turned round and bent over my chair, deliberately flaunting her naked, dimpled buttocks at Frankie whilst she busied herself in unzipping my flies.

'I gasped as she pulled out my prick and took the limp shaft between her lips and began nibbling away with her little white teeth. At the same time Craig slipped off his jacket and stood up behind her. He passed his hand lightly across her bare bottom and then lifted his arm and began slapping her soft bum cheeks. Thwack,

thwack, thwack! He was smacking her firmly but not too hard, and I craned my head across to see her backside change colour from white to pink as she wriggled from side to side. My cock was now as stiff as a poker and I clutched wildly at her hair as Debbie drew back my foreskin and made my helmet swell and bound in her hand whilst she opened her mouth and swirled her tongue all round my knob. Then she began to suck hard, taking almost all of my rigid rod down her throat whilst she let her hands play with my dangling balls.

'Sod me, Ivor, Debbie's one of the best gobblers I've ever come across! She kept her lips taut on my length, licking and lapping in long, rolling sucks and young Frankie now stopped smacking her luscious backside and was busy unbuttoning his jeans. When he was naked, he brandished his big boner in one hand as he parted her bum cheeks with the other.

'"Don't go up my botty," she wailed and Frankie's face clearly showed his disappointment. "Oh go on, Debs, you know what they say, *one up the bum will make you come*."

'"No, I've told you before that I don't like it," she said firmly. "But you can fuck my pussy doggy-style, that would be lovely."

'Naturally, I would have taken Debbie's part if Frankie had ignored her request, but despite his youth, he behaved like a true gentleman and didn't try and force the girl into something she wasn't happy to do. The sight of his thick prick slewing into Debbie's cunt from behind soon made me shoot my load, though when she felt my tadger begin to twitch she started to suck my shaft even harder, and when the gush of jism surged out of my cock, she gulped down my sticky seed, smacking her lips as she drained every drop of jism out of my tool.

'Frankie now pounded away faster and faster and he bent forward and cupped her breasts in his hands, rubbing the brown nippies up to new peaks of hardness as he pumped his rampant tool in and out of her squishy love funnel. Debbie and I cuddled together as I relished the sight of the lad's large cock sliding along the crevice between her bum cheeks as she quivered with every stroke of his gleaming cock.

'She felt behind her until her fingers came into contact with his tight, hairy bollocks and she gently squeezed them as her bum responded to every one of his mighty shoves, exciting her to such raging peaks of lust and then finally over the top as she screamed out: "Yes, yes, yes! Oooh, what a lovely big come! Shoot your spunk Frankie! Give me all you've got!"

'He duly obliged, panting away until he started to shake all over, and with a hoarse cry he shot what must have been a torrent of hot cock cream inside her willing cunt. Debbie let out a loud shriek and closed her legs so that she could contract her cunny muscles and milk him of his last drains of cum as he slumped forward, resting his head on her back for a few moments before he withdrew his now limp, glistening shaft from between her bum cheeks and sank back exhausted on to the sofa. Then when we'd recovered we went upstairs to the bedroom and fucked ourselves silly till almost three in the morning. I fucked Debbie whilst she plated

Frankie and then she sucked us both off at the same time and we finished off by my tit-fucking her whilst Frankie licked her out.

Ivor whistled softly and murmured somewhat unctuously, considering that he had fucked Debbie only about an hour before: 'Wow, you surprise me, Craig, I'd never have realised that she's such a wild girl.'

'Debbie's wild all right,' declared Craig grimly. 'And she's also fun to be with and I'm genuinely sorry I've upset her. But we've had several sessions like that since then, not only with Frankie but also with a randy girlfriend of hers called Claire, and only last Wednesday night, whilst I was fucking Debbie doggy-style as she lay over the arm of the sofa, Claire walks in out of the blue and begins sucking my balls! Debbie hadn't told me that Claire had come round but I didn't kick up a fuss.

'So the long and the short of it is that I honestly believed that Debbie would like it if Harry joined in for an unexpected threesome, and I was staggered when she began sounding off about what a so-and-so I was and how she wouldn't let me or anyone else take her for granted.'

Craig leaned back in his chair and shrugged his shoulders. 'So there we are, boss, that's a very long answer to a short question and I hope that it's cleared the air,' he said with a heartfelt sigh.

'Of course it has,' said Ivor heartily as he rose from his chair and stretched out his right arm to pat Craig lightly on the back. 'Now you've told me the full facts of the matter, I can well understand how this unfortunate misunderstanding occurred, and I'm even more sure that if you apologise to Debbie for what she sees as putting her in an awkward position, the whole business will soon be sorted out and you'll be able to resume what must be a very passionate physical relationship.'

'So you still think I was wrong not to have asked her permission before bringing Harry into the game?' queried Craig.

Ivor looked at him straight in the eye before replying with a small smile playing about his lips: 'Frankly, old boy, yes I do. Whilst I accept you meant no harm, you *assumed* what she would want and in my experience, no girl likes to be thought of as easy-to-please.'

Craig thought hard for a few moments and then smiled and said: 'Okay, Ivor, I hear what you say – I'll go down on my knees to Debbie later this afternoon with a big bunch of flowers and, if she'll let me, I'll take her out for a slap-up dinner.'

'Good lad, that's bound to do the trick,' said Ivor approvingly. 'Now to business – what have you got for me about any competition for this new keep-your-cock-up cream?'

'There are no rival products on the mainstream market,' replied Craig as he shuffled through his papers. 'But in some of the mail order magazines, I've come across something called *Hard Man* which according to this advert from *Reveille* promises to stoke the boiler. It says: "Buy *Hard Man*, a brand new lotion from America, keep yourself up to the mark. *Hard Man* will allow you to control your body and turn those precious minutes into hours of splendid fun!"

'In one of these men's magazines you can only get around Soho or under the counter, the ad gets a bit fruitier – "*Hard Man* helps you get it up for those marvellous marathon love-making sessions. Watch how a little dab will put a smile on her face."'

'How much are they selling it for? And have we any idea who's importing the stuff?' asked Ivor.

'It's quite pricey – two quid for a small tube. God knows who's bringing it in. The firm's called Pleasure Pals Ltd, but the only address in the ads is to where the punters send their cash, and that's just a Post Office Box number address in Birmingham. And before you say any more, I've already written away for a tube.'

Ivor gave him the thumbs-up sign. 'Gold star, Mr Grey – though I hope you didn't put my name and address on the order!'

'Of course not, I used Martin's!' laughed Craig and then added hastily: 'No, not really, though the thought did cross my mind! I bet that more than half the guys replying use aliases when they write in! Mind you, I've done the same. I've sent these people a postal order and used my home address, but I've called myself Mr Oscar Didsbury. I do this quite often when we need to get samples, and so the postman's used to this strange name occasionally appearing on the mail for my flat!'

'Fine, let's just hope Pleasure Pals don't use one of those new franking machines which also prints a little advert on the envelope,' said Ivor wickedly. 'Now is there anything else on the market I should know about?'

'Not really, Ivor, the only other related products are various apparatus for penis enlargement,' Craig replied with a grin as he handed Ivor a cutting from a magazine. 'I don't know whether any of them work, but look at this one from *Pin Up Parade*. I like their style, don't you?'

Ivor examined the advertisement and slowly read aloud: "'Doctor Max says that your erection is caused by blood flowing into the hollow caverns inside your penis. These caverns fill with blood as your penis swells up, but regular use of *Titan* will make these caverns expand, and I guarantee that *Titan* will increase the size of your penis to its maximum dimensions. You'll see the astonishing results the first time you use it and, after regular use, you'll find that these size gains don't disappear." Crikey, what are you supposed to do to stretch your shaft? Do you tie an iron weight on the end of your knob or what?'

Craig shook his head and replied: 'No, I don't think so, it's more likely to be some kind of vacuum device. And I wouldn't be surprised if there were enough men who were worried enough about the size of their dicks to pay five guineas for something like *Titan*.'

'Yes, you're probably right,' Ivor agreed and added thoughtfully: 'Let's face it, despite what they say that once on jack, most cocks measure roughly the same, psychologically speaking, if you're cursed with a small cock, it can be a real downer,' said Ivor pensively.

'You must remember when you were at school how after games the first chaps to strip off for the showers were the ones with the thickest pricks which flapped around so impressively between their legs.'

The telephone rang and Ivor picked up the receiver. 'Hello, Suzie? What's that? Fine, Craig and I will come up to the boardroom straight away.'

Craig looked at his watch and said anxiously: 'Our visitors aren't here yet, are they? It's only half past eleven and they're not due till noon.'

'No, don't worry, but Suzie's prepared the board-room and I think we should have a final council-of-war with her before Messrs Seed and Hynek arrive.'

The two men gathered up their papers and walked up the single flight of stairs to Cable Publicity's conference room, where Suzie was waiting to greet them. Ivor looked approvingly at the notepads and ball-point pens she had put out, along with small bottles of mineral water and glasses which she had placed in front of every chair. 'Well done, love, we'll look the part if nothing else,' he grunted as he sat himself down at the head of the table. 'Have you booked a table at Aldo's?'

'Yes, no problem, he's reserved a nice, quiet table in one of the alcoves,' replied Suzie and then, as she peered over Craig's shoulder to look at the sheaf of advertisements he had taken out of one of his folders and was dividing into little neat piles in front of him, she burst into laughter. 'My God, have you seen these crazy ads, Ivor? Just listen to this – "Would you like to thrill and excite your partner? No matter what size you are, you will gain up to four inches in seventy-two hours or your money will be promptly refunded." Don't you two ever dare to tell me that women are more gullible than men!'

Craig smiled broadly and said: 'Hold on a sec, Suzie, what about all those girls who go for those ads which promise to show flat-chested girls how they can add six inches to their bustlines?'

Suzie grimaced and returned his grin. '*Touché, ma brave*, women are as obsessed with the size of their tits in the same way as men are with the size of their wedding tackle. But at least we girls know how much you men get excited by big boobs whilst I don't know of any female who cares a damn about the measurements of her boyfriend's equipment.'

'Oh, come on, Suzie don't tell us that a big thick prick doesn't turn you on,' Ivor interjected, complacent in the knowledge that his prick might not be the most massive organ in the world but at least it compared well enough in size with most of the other flaccid dicks in the changing room of his squash club.

'I'm not denying anything, but all I'm saying is that when they're ready for action, there isn't much to choose between what most men have between their legs. It's fun to guess, though, whether a new boyfriend is going to have something special to show me when I dip my fingers in his flies. A girlfriend of mine has a theory that you can estimate the size of a boy's dick by looking at his fingers: long straight fingers equals a long straight shaft, short stubby fingers equals a short stubby cock and so on. You haven't done any research on that subject, have you, Craig? I don't have enough experience to know whether there's anything in what she says.'

'Afraid not, m'dear,' said Craig, shaking his head. 'Though if we get this new account and we have to conduct such surveys, perhaps you'd like to help me check the results. Mind, it sounds like another of these old wives' tales to me, though I've not heard of this particular one before.'

'It's a new one as far as I'm concerned as well,' said Ivor and he added sagely: 'I've heard of comparing noses and feet but never fingers. On the other hand, why not? Funny, though, how we always like to figure out what's inside a package before we unwrap it.

'Oh blast it, I forgot to go into Martin's office and get some copies of that new company brochure which lists all our services and mentions some of our clients.'

'Well, no matter, I'll go and get them now, shall I?' asked Suzie, but Ivor frowned and heaved himself out of his chair. 'No, you stay here with Craig, I want to wash my hands, anyway, so I'll stroll over and get them.'

He walked out into the passage and popped into the washroom, although he hadn't desperately needed to have a pee. However, Ivor had always followed a maxim given at a meeting at his college one evening by the wealthy industrial tycoon, Lord Gewirtz, who had advised his audience always to pay a visit to the cloakroom before any kind of important engagement and make themselves as spruce as possible before sitting down at an interview or a conference, because a little extra touch of self-confidence can make all the difference between success and failure.

When he had finished, Ivor made his way to the managing director's office and opened the door to find Patsy, Martin Reese's new junior secretary, standing at his desk with a pile of papers in her hand which she dropped as she whirled round to see who had come in. Three or four sheets of paper fluttered out of her grasp and she pouted angrily: 'Fuck it, I'd just got that bloody Webb file into order,' she said as she squatted down into a bunny-girl dip to pick them up from the floor.

'Sorry, Patsy, I didn't mean to startle you,' apologised Ivor as his eyes ran up and down the figure of the sexy nineteen-year-old girl. Patsy Moss was a genuine eye-turner, with masses of strawberry blonde hair which she wore piled up on her head, and Ivor found himself gazing at her pretty face whose bright blue eyes and full red lips were now drawn into an expression of welcome.

'That's okay, Ivor, it'll only take a few seconds to put these letters back in their folder,' she said sweetly as she ruffled through the papers to slip the offending correspondence into its proper place. 'Now, what can I do for you?'

He was sorely tempted to give an unexpected if utterly truthful answer to this question, for Patsy was wearing a white sweater which emphasised the swell of her rounded breasts which thrust forward so proudly beneath it and the lower half of her shapely figure was encased by a tiny pair of skin tight navy blue hot pants, whilst her legs were covered by matching blue tights, and his cock was beginning to rear in his boxer shorts at this vision of teenage lust.

But although he was dying to direct the conversation to a point when he could ask Patsy if she were free for lunch or a drink after work one day this week, Ivor realised that time was pressing and instead he simply enquired whether she knew where Martin kept the company brochures for prospective clients.

'Of course,' Patsy answered, walking across to a free-standing filing cabinet and, when she bent down to open one of the lower drawers, she gave Ivor a mouth-watering sight of her superb pert buttocks. 'How many would you like?'

'I'll take a handful, if I may,' he said, and as she looked in the drawer for the leaflets, Ivor silently agreed with the thought that Patsy's voluptuous bum cheeks would make a far more interesting handful than Martin's expensively produced brochures!

She straightened herself up and handed Ivor a brown paper packet. 'There are twenty-five in there, Ivor. Will that be enough for you?'

Ivor tore open the package and extracted three brochures. 'That's more than enough, thanks,' he said and then he smiled at the sumptuous girl and went on: 'Patsy, would you be an angel and take the rest of these down to Suzie's office some time today? We've got a meeting with a couple of prospective clients in about twenty minutes and she'll probably be tied-up with me most of the day.'

'Suzie's a lucky girl,' commented Patsy, and looking Ivor straight in the eye, she stepped towards him and added: 'I wouldn't mind being tied-up to you any time.'

Standing now only inches in front of him, Patsy took hold of the package of brochures from Ivor's hands and placed it on the desk. 'I mean what I say, Ivor, I'm a genuine Wysiwyg.'

This sounded extremely interesting, but Ivor was puzzled by the final word. 'A wysiwyg?' Ivor repeated blankly.

Patsy leaned across to whisper in his ear: 'What you see is what you get,' and then she let the tip of her tongue flick across the lobe of his ear. 'And I hope that's true of the bulge I can feel pressing against my tummy.'

As if in a trance, Ivor cradled her thrilling young body in his arms and as their bodies crushed together, she raised her pretty face to his and planted a firm, wet kiss on his lips. Ivor responded avidly, and their tongues slid easily into each other's mouths as she pressed herself uninhibitedly against his raging erection. Then Patsy broke away from the embrace and skipped quickly to the door, which she locked, and as she walked back to Ivor she pulled her sweater over her head, throwing it across a chair, and then she unhooked her half cup bra, baring her firm young breasts as it fluttered onto the carpet.

A choking sound came from Ivor's mouth and for

a brief moment he thought about what might happen if the prospective new clients arrived early. To hell with them, he answered himself as Patsy reached up and untied the knot in his tie before unbuttoning his shirt. With their mouths still locked together and their tongues frantically exploring each other's mouths, he let his jacket slide off his shoulders and, like magnets, his hands shot forward to caress the soft, rounded spheres of Patsy's breasts and when he rubbed the elongated red nipples against his palms, she groaned with excitement.

They continued to shed their clothes until they were both completely naked and then they slowly sank down in a tangle of limbs onto the thick, pale green carpet. There was neither the time nor inclination for foreplay and Ivor growled with desire when Patsy lay on her back and spread her legs wide apart. The musk of female passion assailed his nostrils and Ivor's shaft positively ached with desire as he straddled the nubile girl and gazed upon her beautiful breasts which lolled seductively with their big, swollen nipples pointing prettily away from each other. Then he looked down further at the thatch of curly brown hair covering her crotch, and through which he could clearly see the pink edges of her cunny that were already glistening with sensual anticipation.

'What are you waiting for, Ivor?' Patsy murmured throatily. 'Go ahead and fuck me, I've wanted you to screw me ever since I started this job.'

She held his cock tightly and guided his knob between her yielding love lips. Ivor thrust his shaft inside her to the hilt and stayed still, delighting in the delicious sensation of Patsy's cunny walls clinging to his pulsating prick. Their bodies were now joined from mouth to groin and his broad chest crushed against her nipples. So tightly were their bodies glued together that Ivor felt as if his penis had been welded inside her juicy wet cunt.

He began to move his hips backwards and forwards as he started to fuck this gorgeous girl, pistoning his prick in to the very root with each downward thrust whilst Patsy raised her bottom sharply to meet him, forcing every last millimetre of his hot, twitching tool inside her. She wrapped her legs around his waist and panted: 'Aaah! Aaah! What a lovely thick cock you have, Ivor, and I know it's loaded with jism. Go on, we haven't got enough time for you to wait for me. Let me have it, big boy, I can take all you've got. Come on, shoot it all up my cunt! Fill me to the brim with your creamy cum, you randy bugger!'

Not surprisingly, Ivor needed no further urging and he speeded up the rhythm of his fucking until with a deep groan he thundered into her in a powerful frenzy, and his cock sent a fountain of pent-up spunk deep inside her irresistible honeypot.

Patsy caressed his head as he lay upon her, gasping for air as he recovered from his climax and said encouragingly: 'M'mm, that was good, very good – a nice thick cock inside my pussy really sets me up for the day! Could you come in early, Ivor, and then I'll have time to come as well. But please do me a favour and don't tell Martin that I like a good fuck, because although he's awfully sweet, I don't fancy him half as much as I fancy you, and besides, he's screwing Carole whenever he gets the chance.'

Mention of time made Ivor scramble to his feet and frantically begin to pull on his clothes. 'I'd love to,' he said as he buttoned his shirt. 'And you must forgive me for dashing off so quickly but these new clients will be here any minute. Well, not exactly here, Suzie'll be taking them to the boardroom, though if I showed them into this office and they saw you like you are now, I bet we'd sign them up on the spot!'

'Thanks for the compliment, Ivor,' she said, stretching her nubile young body out on the carpet and smiling wantonly at him whilst she let her hand stray across her hairy notch. 'Now Martin is going to Manchester to see Paul Evans this evening and he'll be staying there for a couple of days, so if you want to keep yourself in my good books, be here at quarter to nine tomorrow morning and we'll take things up from where we left off.'

'I'll be here, don't you worry,' promised Ivor as the telephone rang and he picked up the receiver whilst he slipped his feet into his Bally moccasins. 'Hello, Martin Reese's office. Oh, Suzie, hi there, love. Yes, go down to reception and bring them up to the boardroom. I was just on my way over when you called.'

He turned to Patsy who had stood up whilst he was answering Suzie's call and was busily pulling up her panties. 'The new clients have arrived so I must go,' said Ivor regretfully. 'If I don't see you before, I'll see you early tomorrow morning.'

'Be on time, Ivor,' she warned with a saucy grin on her cheeky face. 'For if you're late, I'll have to start without you and that wouldn't be so nice for either of us, would it?'

'I'll be here on the dot,' he promised as he dashed out of the office and walked briskly down the corridor towards the boardroom.

TWO

A Lunch To Remember

Ivor paused, straightened his tie and took a deep breath before opening the door of the boardroom, but though Craig Grey stood up as he entered the room, there was no sign of Suzie or their visitors.

'Hello, Ivor, where have you been?' asked Craig as he slumped back into his seat. 'I thought you were only popping across to get a couple of brochures from Martin's office. You must have taken the scenic route.'

'Not really, it took a while for Patsy to find them and then I had to make a quick call to Tony Mulliken about the Ruff Trayde situation. You know that his latest record hasn't exactly hit the heights,' said Ivor unblinkingly as he took his place at the head of the table.

His entrance was well-timed, for seconds later Suzie threw open the door and announced: 'Mr Seed and Mr Hynek for you, Mr Belling.'

Ivor dragged himself up and walked across the room and extended his hand to a fair-haired man in his early thirties. 'Keith Seed? How do you do, I'm Ivor Belling and these are my colleagues, Craig Grey, who's in charge of our market research division and this is my other personal assistant, Suzie Harrison, who you've already met.'

'Good to meet you, Mr Belling,' said Keith Seed as he shook hands with Ivor and Craig. 'And let me introduce my partner, Bennie Hynek, all the way from sunny Israel.'

'Nice to meet you, Mr Hynek,' said Ivor, his smile slightly faltering as his hand was crushed in an iron grip by a broad giant of a man whose bronzed good looks had already been noted by Suzie when she had escorted Cable's guests up to the boardroom.

'I'm very much looking forward to this meeting,' said the Israeli in a deep, masculine voice with only the slightest trace of a foreign accent. 'If the claims that Martin Reese was making to us were not too exaggerated, I think we could be involved in a very profitable partnership together.'

Ivor waved them to their seats as he replied: 'That's the best kind of relationship, isn't it, when both sides gain out of working together. I'm sorry that Martin can't be here till later but if, as I hope, you'll join us for lunch, he'll meet us at the restaurant.'

'Yes, that'll be fine. Actually, he rang me this morning to confirm this would be okay,' said Keith Seed.

'Good, in that case, let's get straight down to business.' said Ivor. 'Perhaps the best way to begin is if you would like to tell us all about this new magic cream which will enable those who need help to stand up and be counted.'

'*Sus tza'era* is not a magic cream, Mr Belling,'

interrupted Bennie Hynek with a frown. 'Nor do we claim it to be an aphrodisiac in the strict meaning of the word. The cream is a scientific combination of herbal ingredients which assists the natural functions of the male body and this is why it can help men who have experienced sexual problems to gain and maintain penile erections.'

Ivor nodded slowly and said: 'Well, that's wonderful news for those suffering from such terrible complaints – please forgive me if I sounded sceptical, but earlier on Craig showed me some advertisements put out by your competitors and, frankly, I wasn't very impressed by the look of them.'

'No, don't apologise, you were right to feel cynical about the claims of some of these fly-by-night merchants,' said Keith Seed as he brought out a paper from his document case. 'But as Bennie has said, unlike some of these spurious pills and potions, we are offering a genuine product. Now I cannot reveal the make-up of the cream to you – I'm not certain of all the ingredients myself – but I'd like you to read this letter from Professor Bernard Gottlieb who is the distinguished head of medical research at Shmekel Laboratories in Tel Aviv which manufactures *Sus tza'era*.'

He passed the letter over to Ivor and Craig asked: 'What does *Sus tza'era* mean in English, Mr Hynek?'

'It's Hebrew for Young Horse, and Keith suggests that in Britain we should also call it something similar like *Stallion*,' translated the big Israeli as Ivor studied the letter which stated:

To Whom It May Concern

Sus tza'era is a preparation designed to produce an instant erection when rubbed on the glans or head of the penis. It is made up of a compound which comprises Dead Sea salt and a number of totally harmless herbal ingredients manufactured into an orange flavoured fruit base. Whilst no guarantees can be given as to its efficacy in all cases, a great improvement in potency was recorded by more than eighty per cent of patients in a three-month series of strictly monitored laboratory tests.

'That's a pretty impressive testimonial,' said Ivor as he passed on the letter to Craig. 'May we keep it?'

'Of course, as you see it's only a photocopy of the original, but doesn't it show how we can give a new dimension of sexual pleasures to those who thought they were past it,' said Keith Seed who was obviously extremely taken with the idea of bringing the product to Europe. 'Let me just add that how *Sus tza'era* or *Stallion*, which I think we should keep at least as a working title, does its job is that when rubbed briskly on to your old man, it causes a flow of blood to rush into your shaft and, hey presto, an instant fulfilling erection which won't go down before you've even begun and you're ready, willing and able to fuck the nearest pussy to hand.'

He looked triumphantly around the table and caught Suzie's eye which made him flush. 'Oh dear, I hope I haven't embarrassed you,' he said to her, but Suzie gave a short laugh and assured him that on the contrary, she was extremely interested in what had been said. 'I was telling Ivor only this morning how one of my boyfriends suffers from the 'hair-trigger' syndrome. Tell me, does your cream also keep the penis hard and stiff for a longer period of time?'

'Yes, it will definitely help delay a man's orgasm, though not necessarily until his partner is ready for him to climax. However, for those men with bad cases of premature ejaculation, Shmekel Laboratories have also prepared a special desensitizing lubricant called *Arrest*,' replied Bennie Hynek and he looked straight at Suzie with a twinkle in his blue eyes and went on: 'This is an invisible, unscented gel which I'm sure will solve your friend's problem.'

'Does the stuff really work?' wondered Suzie and he nodded his head and instantly replied: 'Well, Miss Suzie, all I can tell you is that it certainly cured my own particular disorder!'

'You had trouble keeping control? I have to say that I find that rather hard to believe,' said Suzie, looking saucily at the handsome Israeli.

'Nevertheless, I promise you that this was the case,' he assured her with great emphasis. 'Why, I'll tell you about it if you're interested.'

Suzie looked at Ivor who smiled and gave her a quick wink and said: 'Well, Mr Hynek, if you're sure you don't mind . . .'

'Not in the slightest,' he said and flashing Suzie a smile he went on: 'It all happened about eighteen months ago when I was doing my four weeks annual army service on a kibbutz deep in the Negev Desert, whose members manufactured furniture in a big

65

workshop as well as raising chickens and growing fruit in specially irrigated fields. All Israelis have to do this every year, you know, until we reach the age of forty-nine or until the Arabs finally stop trying to drive us into the sea.

'However, I would be the first to admit that being sent to kibbutz Natan Horowitz was an easy posting as far as I and the other reservists were concerned. After all, we were too far away from the Egyptian and Jordanian borders for any Arab terrorists to trouble us, and I looked forward to four weeks' holiday guarding the perimeter of the kibbutz with my colleagues. Anyhow, it was very, very hot during the day and there was no shade when we went out on patrol around the barbed-wire fences. I could hardly wait till one of my friends came along to relieve me and I decided to go straight to the swimming pool and cool off.

'It was three o'clock in the afternoon and, as I had guessed, there was nobody around for all the kibbutzniks were hard at work. I put down my rifle, stripped off my uniform and then I paused for about thirty seconds, savouring the freedom of standing naked in the sunshine before slipping on my swimming trunks and diving straight into the water. I splashed around for a while and then when I climbed out and looked around, I noticed that I had been mistaken for there was one person there, a girl named Julie who was one of the three beautiful blonde Danish girls who were staying in the kibbutz guest-house before travelling down to Eilat. She had caught my eye during supper the previous evening when she and her friends had sat at my table, and now here she was, sunbathing topless on a mattress with her lovely big breasts glistening in the sun as she lay stretched out on her back.

'It occurred to me that Julie must have seen me stand naked just before, but what the heck. I walked over to her and said: "Hi, are you having a good rest? I wouldn't spend too much time in the sun if I were you or you might burn."

'"*Todah*, Bennie, I think I'd better take your advice," she replied as she sat up, her pretty breasts swinging from side to side as she draped a towel around her neck.

'"You must be very careful with your colouring, Julie," I said as I noticed her staring at the mountainous bulge in the front of my swimming costume. "Here, let me take your mattress over to the other side of the pool where you can lie under the shade of that clump of trees."

'She followed me as I hauled the mattress round the pool and thanked me again as she put down her bag and spread her towel upon the mattress. Then as I was about to leave her, Julie lifted her finger and beckoned me back to her. I still had a raging hard-on but I walked straight back towards her, for there was no way I could even attempt to conceal the obvious bulge in my swimming trunks. However, as it transpired, it was this protuberance in my crotch which interested her because, when I came up to stand directly in front of her, Julie smiled sexily up at me and said softly: "Bennie, did you know that I am a medical student?"

'"No, I didn't," I replied as she placed her palm on my straining shaft and asked if she could see for herself what was causing such a large swelling between my legs – and then without waiting for an answer, Julie ripped my costume down to my ankles and my naked erection sprung up to greet her as she grasped my quivering cock in her hands, running her fingertips all along its length.

'Julie knelt on the mattress and licked all round the top of my prick and I uttered a heartfelt moan of pure pleasure. "Doesn't that feel good, my big soldier?" she whispered, and all I could do was nod my head for these marvellous sensations were making me speechless.

'"Yes, I thought you'd like that," she said softly as she continued to slide her hand up and down my throbbing tool. "Well, now that I've switched on the gas, I suppose I had better light the fire," and with these words she opened her mouth and sucked in my knob between her lips. Julie's head bobbed back and forth as she proceeded to give me the most wonderful oral fuck I had ever experienced. I closed my eyes and let the warm waves of ecstasy flow all over my body and then, all of a sudden, I felt the sperm surge through my shaft and fly down her throat. She swallowed all my cum and when my ejaculation was over she swirled her tongue all over my semi-limp cock as I withdrew it from her mouth.

'"Wow, that didn't last very long, I suppose you boys don't get the chance to screw around very much when you're on active service," she said as she stood up and peeled off her bikini bottoms before lying down on her back. "But at least you can repay the compliment and eat my pussy."

'"With pleasure," I replied, not only because I enjoy cunnilingus but because I hoped that my cock would recover its strength whilst I brought Julie off with my tongue. Anyhow, I carefully lowered myself on top of her, positioning myself until my tongue was level with her big, brown nipples and I leaned my head forward and began to nibble them between my lips, gently nipping them with my teeth until she was moaning with pleasure and then I let my tongue travel slowly down across the smooth, warm skin of her belly and into the fluffy blonde pussy curls between her legs. Like a snake, I slid my head between her thighs and when I leaned forward to kiss her pussy, she immediately clamped her thighs around my neck.

'I was in no hurry to bring Julie off and I began by running my finger back and forth along the length of her juicy crack and massaging the tiny erect clitty which was peeping out of its hood.

'"A-a-a-h, that's wonderful," she cried as I now started to lick her pussy lips which were already hot and sticky with her tangy love juice, and as I lapped at her fragrant cunt I felt her sigh and tremble, her breath catching in little ragged gasps of delight.

'"Now I worked my tongue inside the long gash of her slit and I slipped one of my hands underneath her bottom to press her cunt even closer to me as I placed my lips directly over her clitty and sucked it into my mouth. I could feel it growing larger as Julie's heels drummed against the mattress and she became wildly agitated when I found the button under the fold at the base of her clitty and began twirling my tongue around it. The faster I vibrated my tongue, the more she heaved and bucked from side to side and I was hard pressed to keep her pussy pressed against my face.

"'H-a-a-a-r! H-a-a-a-r! Stick your cock in me now, Bennie!" she screamed out as she unlocked my head from its prison between her thighs. I scrambled up and she grabbed hold of my shaft which was heavy but not fully erect, though when she grabbed my tool and began pumping her hand up and down its slippery length, it soon swelled up to bursting point. I raised myself up and thrust my cock inside her to the hilt and her cunny was so wet and yet so tight that I felt as if my prick had been welded inside her cunt.

"'Oh, I'm so *full*!" she gasped as she crossed her legs over the small of my back. "Fuck me hard, soldier boy, I want every inch of your big, fat joystick. Stuff it right up my cunt."

'I was only too happy to give Julie what she wanted! I plunged my prick into her love hole with all the energy I could muster and I sucked on her nipples whilst I fucked her, my balls banging against her bottom as I drove my pulsating penis in and out of her squelchy honeypot. All too soon, though, my body began to tremble and the sensations were so strong and so wild that despite my frantic efforts to hold back, I was forced to surrender to my orgasm and shot a fountain of spunk into the long funnel of Julie's cunt as her body twisted and writhed underneath me.

"'Hey, what's the rush?" she panted with her arms

round me as I lay on top of her. "Have you got another appointment or something, Bennie? If you don't have to rush away, though, let's rest a while and then next time hold on and wait for me." '

The memory of this encounter made Bennie Hynek sigh and he smiled ruefully at Suzie who had been listening attentively to every word of his story before he continued: 'Well, the upshot was that half an hour later I made love to Julie again, but again I came far too quickly and had to finish her off with my fingers. I didn't worry too much about the incident at first, but when I returned home after finishing my army service, I found that the same thing was happening with my girlfriend. For some reason I was coming far too quickly and the problem was getting worse the more I worried about what was happening to me. A friend told me to try ginseng capsules, but these had no effect and I was beginning to wonder if I would ever again be able to satisfy a woman.

'Then I saw an advertisement for *Sus tza'era* in a newspaper and sent away for a tube. I used the cream for about six weeks and since then I've had no trouble at all when I make love. In fact, nowadays when I make love to one of my girlfriends I am often complimented on my staying power. You must excuse me if this sounds boastful, but it is nothing but the truth.'

He looked triumphantly around the table and Ivor said: 'Well, that's a good enough recommendation for anybody. Unless you have any objections, Mr Hynek, I think it would be a good idea to print your anecdote – changing the names of those involved, of course – on a sheet of paper inside every box of *Stallion*. By the way, I don't think you'll find a better name for the product, do you, Craig?'

'No, I think that *Stallion* fits the bill,' murmured his colleague, who was watching with interest how Bennie and Suzie were smiling at each other and how their eyes were locked together in a gaze of mutual admiration.

'Ivor, why don't I now go through some projected start-up facts and figures which might help our friends decide which way they wish to follow regarding the marketing of *Stallion*,' suggested Craig as he pulled out some papers from one of his files.

'Good idea,' said Ivor approvingly, 'and then we can adjourn to Aldo's for a spot of lunch.'

Craig Grey's presentation was a great success, and Ivor could see that both of the prospective clients were impressed with the way Craig marshalled all the facts they needed to know before embarking on their project.

And equally impressive was the delicious meal at Aldo's restaurant which was situated in Bresslaw Street, barely a five-minute walk from Cable Publicity's offices. After their starters, Aldo had insisted they order the day's specials – fresh asparagus soup followed by poached salmon plaited with sole in a herb butter sauce with new potatoes and a panache of fresh vegetables – saying to Ivor in his best stage Italian (though he was born and bred in nearby Camberwell): 'If you donna like, Signor Belling, you can have-a da meal on the house.'

By the time the waiter came round with the dessert trolley, the Cable team were on first name terms with their new clients, and Bennie Hynek and Suzie had struck up such an especially close relationship that Ivor was hardly surprised when he heard his secretary agree to meet the handsome and sophisticated former paratrooper for a drink after work that night.

Ivor insisted that everyone join him for a cognac or some other liqueur when the waiter asked if they would prefer expresso or cappucino coffees to finish their meal. 'It's almost three years to the day since I joined Cable Publicity, Keith,' he explained, and Craig and Keith Seed accepted his invitation and Suzie ordered a cointreau and Bennie Hynek asked if he could have a kummel.

'My old grandfather, who emigrated to Israel in the nineteén-thirties from Czechoslovakia, always drank a glass of Kummel on Saturday nights when the Sabbath ended, and I've inherited his taste for the drink,' he said to Suzie whilst the waiter scurried off to find out whether Aldo kept the liqueur in stock.

'I can't say I've ever heard of kummel. What's it made from?' Craig enquired and Bennie explained: 'It comes from Central Europe and is distilled from caraway seeds, which tastes very nice and is also very good for the digestion.'

Aldo did indeed keep kummel in his cellar and came to their table himself with the wine waiter to produce the bottle with a theatrical flourish. 'Who is the gentleman who ordered kummel?' he demanded as he poured a generous measure into a glass. 'I will have one with you, signor, as I'm playing golf at my club this afternoon.'

'What the blazes has that got to do with it, Aldo?' asked Ivor curiously.

'Ah, you're obviously not a golfer, Signor Belling, or you would know that kummel is known as "putting mixture" by the professionals. They swear that a small glass of kummel before you start a round will steady your nerves when you reach the green. I'm afraid it hasn't yet worked so far as I am concerned, but it's still a good excuse for a drink!'

At this stage Martin Reese made his delayed appearance. 'Hello there, everybody, how are things going?' he asked as he pulled up a chair. 'I hope that Ivor and Craig have been good hosts in my absence.'

'They've been absolutely splendid,' said Keith Seed. 'In fact, to be quite blunt, Martin, we haven't missed you at all! We've all the information we need to go ahead, haven't we, Bennie?'

'Yes, if Keith agrees, I would like to appoint your company to work on our behalf when we launch *Stallion*,' said Bennie Hynek, glancing at his partner who nodded his head in agreement. 'You've already discussed your fees with Keith, Martin, and I don't think we'll quarrel about those too much. But I would like an assurance that Ivor and Craig will be working on our account and you won't give our business to any junior executives.'

'By all means, Bennie, though you must appreciate that though Ivor will be in charge of your account, he will have to appoint someone else to handle all the day-to-day business,' he promised, and the Israeli nodded and said: 'Sure, that's perfectly okay and I'd like to suggest that Suzie here is on our team.' He turned to her and said: 'You wouldn't mind working on our behalf, would you?'

'I'd love it, if it's okay with my boss,' she said promptly, looking across at Ivor who gave a wide grin and said: 'That's okay with me, Suzie, I'm sure the publicity campaign will benefit from a feminine view as how best we should pitch our message to all those wives and girlfriends whose partners are having problems in bed.'

'That's all settled then,' said Keith Seed, reaching across the table to shake hands with the members of his newly appointed agency. 'Now, this calls for a celebration. Signor Aldo, have you a bottle of champagne on ice?'

'Si, Signor, of course we always chill some bottles every morning for the lunchtime trade,' said the restauranteur. 'Franco, bring a bottle of the Moet and Chandon '64 from the fridge downstairs.'

'No arguments, Ivor, this is on me,' insisted Keith Seed, as he took out his wallet and beckoned Aldo over to his side. 'How much is that, please?'

He paid Aldo for the champagne, which Franco produced at top speed, and even after toasting the forthcoming launch of *Stallion* in Great Britain, there was enough sparkling wine left to drink to England's chances in the World Cup football matches scheduled for July.

Martin placed his hands on Keith and Bennie's

shoulders. 'Now, how are you two fixed for the rest of this afternoon?' he asked.

The two men exchanged a questioning glance and then Keith said slowly: 'Well, to be frank, in case Cable didn't come up with the goods, we did make a date to pop in and see Mike Harper at Lempert, Tolanski and Stoll in Bloomsbury Square. I suppose we should call them and cancel the appointment.'

'I've got a good idea,' Martin said heartily. 'Ivor can ask my secretary to telephone Mike Harper and pass on your apologies to him whilst you two boys come along with me to my club for a couple of hours. We can dot the i's and cross the t's of the contract over a nice cup of tea, or something stronger if you so fancy.'

Bennie Hynek grunted his approval. 'Very well, Martin, that will be very nice. Now, is it worth taking my car? I've left it round the corner in the new underground car park in Goldhill Square.'

'Best to leave it there, Bennie,' said Martin, rising to his feet. 'We're only going to Mayfair and it's far easier to jump into a taxi. Ivor, please ask Patsy to ring Mike Harper for Keith. We'll be at the Hunkiedorie Club if needed, but I'll be back at the office later as I have a meeting with Lord Lieberman at half past six about helping him publicise his bill to curb pirate radio stations.'

Martin shepherded them out of the restaurant and Craig turned to Ivor and said sarcastically: 'God, it's a hard life being a managing director, isn't it? You have to spend all morning romping in bed with your personal assistant and then rush over to a posh gentlemen's club to see a high class strip show with the most beautiful call-girls in London on hand if you're not too tired for a bit more rumpy-pumpy.'

Suzie cocked her head and said: 'Oh-ho, the cat's out of the bag at last – I didn't realise that the Hunkiedorie was little more than a knocking shop. No wonder you're always entertaining clients there.'

Ivor was stung by this accusation, although he and Martin had both enjoyed the sexual favours of several Hunkiedorie hostesses over the previous twelve months. 'The Hunkiedorie Club isn't a knocking shop, Suzie,' he said stiffly. 'There may be an occasional stag cabaret now and then, but that's as far as it goes.'

'Pull the other one, Ivor, there's much more than striptease going on there,' teased Craig whilst Ivor signed the bill which would be sent on to the agency. 'Martin took me to one of those red-hot stag shows a couple of weeks ago and I've only just recovered from the experience!'

'Sounds interesting,' said Suzie as they said goodbye to Aldo and made their way back to the office. 'I once saw a spectacularly sexy cabaret in Amsterdam, but I didn't think that there were any such shows being put on in London. Was the Hunkiedorie striptease very daring, Craig?'

'Wait till we get back to the boardroom for the debriefing meeting and then I'll gladly tell you all the lurid details,' chuckled Craig and, when they arrived back at the office, they went straight back to the boardroom and Ivor called Patsy on the internal phone to give her Martin's message about cancelling

Keith and Bennie's afternoon date with the rival firm of public relations consultants.

'Come on, Craig, let's hear about your adventures at the Hunkiedorie before we start work again,' urged Suzie, and Ivor noticed that his secretary's cheeks were definitely rather flushed. She was not exactly under the influence but he had seen how Bennie Hynek had kept Suzie's glass filled throughout the meal and this had put her into a merry, mellow mood.

'Suzie, how about a coffee whilst Craig spills the beans? No, don't get up, I'll go to the vending machine downstairs. I've a ton of coppers in my pocket,' said Ivor and he rose up and walked briskly towards the door. 'Black, no sugar for you, isn't that right? Craig, you take your coffee white with one sugar like me, don't you?'

He strolled out and fed the necessary pennies into the vending machine which dispensed paper cups of hot drinks for only twopence. He found a tray and went back into the boardroom where Craig had just explained that Martin had invited him to the Hunkiedorie as a reward for his work on the Four Seasons dog food account.

'The main rooms in the club look very respectable,' he was saying when Ivor entered the room and set down their coffees on the table. 'And we had a superb dinner in the restaurant, but once Martin and I were given the go-ahead by the head waiter to pass through a green door next to the cashier's desk, we were transported into another world.

'On the other side of the door there's a topless bar.

All the waitresses and barmaids were bare-breasted and wore only microscopic white skirts which were semi-transparent, together with black fishnet stockings and high stiletto heels. We sat down and a gorgeous blonde girl with large creamy breasts came over to take our order. She had a circular name tag with 'Kathy' printed on it pinned to the side of her skirt, under which I could clearly make out the outline of her garter belt and a miniscule G-string.

'"Hello, Mr Reese, how's the world treating you?" she said and then she leaned forward and planted a big, wet kiss smack on Martin's forehead.

'"It's not treating me, Kathy, I'm paying for myself as usual," Martin replied as he returned her greeting by nuzzling his lips round one of her big crimson nipples.

'Kathy didn't seem to be put out by this, although she pulled back a foot or so and said: "Stop it, you naughty boy, it's too early to get me all worked up. They'll be plenty of time for that sort of thing later. Now then, what would you and your friend like to drink?"

'Well, we had come to the Hunkiedorie in my car, which the doorman had parked for me, and as I had already had two glasses of wine with dinner, I asked for a Coca-Cola because I never drink and drive, not since my cousin Steve copped a broken arm when he was knocked off his motorbike by a driver who was so pissed that he could hardly stand up when he was pulled out from his car.

'Anyhow, Martin gave me a nudge with his elbow and said: "Are you sure that's all you want, old boy? In this bar, there isn't very much difference in the price of soft drinks and champagne."

'I said: "No, honestly, Martin, a Coke will do me fine, though don't let me stop you," and he winked at Kathy and said: "Don't worry, my lad, there's no danger of that. Well, you heard the man, Kathy, that's just a Coca-Cola and a half bottle of the house bubbly, love."

'Kathy went off to get the drinks, her bum cheeks jiggling from side to side in the tight skirt, and I looked around us. There was a juke-box near us and it was blaring out a Rolling Stones number over the general hubbub. There must have been about forty or fifty customers in the place, which was decorated like a saloon in a Western movie. Mind, you wouldn't see what I saw going on in anything but a blue film. There was a redheaded girl lying on her back on the bar, absolutely stark naked, and a black man was tonguing her pussy as hard as he could. She certainly looked as though she was enjoying herself and I looked on with fascination as she pulled her cunny lips apart so that he could lick her out more easily.

'"Here, I recognise that spade from the papers," said Martin as we watched another girl come up and french-kiss the red-head whilst she squeezed her nipples between her fingers. "I'll bet a pound to a penny that's Chief Elumo Bazuboko, the President of Malumbi. You know who I mean, Craig? He's the guy that's always spouting about the moral decline of the decadent West when he goes over to New York to spout at the United Nations, or when he flies in here to ask for another few million quid in aid."

"'He doesn't look as if he needs any aid just now," I remarked, for President Bazuboko had taken out his tongue from the redheaded girl's pussy and had now relieved himself of his jacket and trousers. With surprising agility for a heavily built man, he climbed onto the bar and to a round of cheers from a group of onlookers standing by the couple, he replaced his tongue with his shiny black prick with which he fucked her at a great rate of knots.

"'Well, you can't say that the Hunkiedorie doesn't do its share to cement good relations between Britain and the Commonwealth," said Martin thoughtfully whilst the President cried out something appropriate in Swahili as he pumped his cum into the willing girl's cunt.

'Kathy now came back with our drinks and said to us: "Here you are, gentlemen, one Coke and one half bottle of champagne. Now would you like to buy some lottery tickets for tonight's draw? They're only a pound each or six for a fiver."

"'What's the prize?" I asked in all innocence which made Kathy giggle and say to Martin: "You obviously haven't been to the Hunkiedorie before, have you? Mr Reese, tell your nice friend about what he can win in our raffles, because I want to sell you both some tickets. Come on, I only have about fifteen left."

'Martin looked a little sheepish and muttered: "The lucky winner gets to be the meat in the sandwich with three of the bar girls, but frankly, Craig, I think the bloody draw's fixed because I've always bought tickets but I've never won since I first came to the Hunkiedorie in 1963!"

"'It's not fixed, honest it's not,'" retorted Kathy indignantly and she tickled me under the chin and said: "Take no notice of him, Craig, perhaps you'll be lucky tonight. It's great fun and it'll be especially worthwhile winning tonight because I'm one of the three girls who'll give the winner a good time that he'll never forget."

'I held back at first and said that whilst the offer was very tempting, I didn't fancy performing in public, but Kathy laid her hand on my shoulder and cooed: "We don't fuck here, you silly-billy, we go into a special little room behind the bar."

"'Oh, well, in that case, I'll have a fiver's worth," I said and Martin grunted: "You're wasting your money, Craig, I'm one hundred per cent positive that the sodding thing's rigged," although I noticed that he still bought three tickets from Kathy!'

Suzie's eyes glinted as she leaned forward over the table and said: 'Don't tell me, Craig, I bet Martin's number came up. Never mind what he says, he's a lucky so-and-so. I happen to know that he won a hundred pounds on the Premium Bonds last November, only a few months after his Mum gave him twenty pounds worth of bonds as a birthday present.'

Craig chuckled and continued: 'Well, his luck wasn't in on this occasion, because the winning ticket drawn out of a hat by Kathy was mine! I could hardly believe it because I'd never won anything before in my life.

But Kathy called me up to the bar and led me into a little room where two of the other girls were waiting for me. They had already taken off their scanty costumes and as soon as Kathy had closed the door, they started to undress me. One was a petite Eurasian girl called Jilly and the other was a plumpish West Indian chick with big breasts and a mass of thick curly hairs round her pussy.

'I was excited at the sight of these gorgeous, naked girls but I was nervous, so much so that I didn't have a hard-on. However, this was put right pretty quickly by the West Indian girl, whose name was Martha, who made me stand up against the wall and then knelt down and began to kiss my cock whilst Kathy slipped off her clothes.

'Soon I was sporting a massive erection which Martha took between her lips and gave me a marvellous 'deep throat' gobble, pushing her head forward until the entire shaft disappeared inside her mouth. Then Jilly dropped down beside her and began to play with my balls and, when she had finished undressing, Kathy kissed me and rubbed her glorious, high-pointed breasts against my chest.

'The idea of having three sexy, nude girls soon sent me over the top and I sent a sticky white fountain of spunk down Martha's throat. But I was now so turned on that my cock stayed hard as Martha gave my knob a final wash before heaving herself up to her feet.

'"We don't have too much time left, so who would you like to fuck, Craig?" asked Jilly. What a hard decision, but Kathy made up my mind for me by saying firmly that because she had sold the winning ticket, she should be given the honour of being fucked by my big thick cock.

'I said that seemed very fair to me and so the girls told me to lie down on the floor and Kathy mounted my rigid prick, sliding gaily up and down on my pulsating pole and hugging my shaft inside her tight, wet honeypot whilst Jilly also straddled me – but higher up my body over my head. She faced Kathy as she crouched over my face and then pressed herself down over my mouth and nose and I licked and lapped around her pussy lips whilst Kathy continued to ride my cock.

'There was no place for Martha, but when I moved Jilly's lovely bum cheeks upwards to give me a chance to breathe more easily, I saw her at my side playing with an enormous pink dildo which she was pushing in and out of her cunny with great enjoyment – not that I was complaining about the state of play! Each time I pushed up into Kathy's love channel her breasts bounced as she leaned backwards, which allowed me to go in even deeper.

'When Kathy sensed I was about to come, she started to ride me like a jockey in sight of the winning post. I moved my hips up and down in time with her rhythm and then my cock spurted out a fierce jet of jism inside her cunt which made Kathy shudder violently as the force of her own climax rocketed through her body whilst I emptied my balls inside her.

'Then I brought Jilly off with my tongue, nibbling her stiff little clitty till she began to gyrate her pelvis as she worked herself off and sent a flood of tangy love juice over my lips and chin.

'"Hey, leave something for me," Martha cried out and the girls moved off my body, but I was out for the count and not even Kathy and Jilly, both sucking my cock, could revive me.'

'Such a pity you didn't have a tube of *Stallion* handy, old boy,' Ivor said solemnly. 'Otherwise you could have carried out some first class empirical research for Bennie and Keith.'

Suzie giggled but Craig clicked his fingers together and exclaimed: 'Yes, Ivor, you're right. It would have been the perfect opportunity to test the product's effectiveness which is very important to know before we begin our publicity campaign. Look here, Bennie's kindly left us a couple of sample tubes so we could start work straight away. All we need are a couple of willing girls who'll help us find out whether *Stallion* really works.'

The two men both glanced at Suzie who was clearly unamused, for she glared at them and pouted angrily: 'What a bloody cheek!'

'Oh, I'm sorry, Suzie. I didn't mean to suggest that you should be one of these two girls,' said Craig hastily.

She tossed back her long, silky tresses of hair and said haughtily: 'It's not that you thought about me taking part in such research, Craig, it's the fact that you should imagine that I needed another girl to help me!'

'Ah, well, that's a quite different matter, of course,' muttered Ivor as he wondered whether it would be wise to continue this conversation which appeared to be leading onto dangerous ground, especially as Craig appeared to have let his normal, cautious, common-sense approach to work desert him, for he had jumped up and run to lock the board-room door.

Ivor quickly resolved that in all probability it would be far wiser to change the subject of debate without delay, but this sensible conclusion was immediately overridden by the burgeoning activity between his legs, where the stiffening shaft of his penis was already beginning to swell menacingly inside his boxer shorts and push through the slit to form a distinctive mound in Ivor's lap.

Sod it, worse things happen at sea, he said consolingly to himself as he watched Suzie stand up and shrug off her blouse and then unzip her skirt which she pulled down over her hips whilst Craig shed his jacket and sat down to fumble with the buttons of his shirt.

'Okay, Ivor, whoever's last to show Suzie his cock buys lunch for all three of us tomorrow,' said Craig encouragingly and this, coupled with the stirring sight of his stunning young secretary releasing her large creamy breasts from the confines of her bra, made any further resistance impossible and with a gulp, Ivor surrendered to the sensuality of the moment and feverishly began to tear off his clothes.

Within sixty seconds all three of them were stark naked and Suzie padded across to a small couch underneath the window and sat down in the centre of the sofa, patting the cushions on either side of her as she said invitingly: 'Come on then, let me take a closer look at your crown jewels.'

Neither of the men were overly embarrassed by seeing the other's erect truncheon, for only a few months ago in Glasgow the two of them had participated in an uninhibited orgy which took place in a swank hotel room after Ivor had summoned Craig up to Scotland to help secure another new account for Cable Publicity.

So they sat themselves down on either side of Suzie, who grabbed hold of their throbbing pricks, sliding the fingers of one hand around Craig's cock and making a fist around Ivor's boner with the fingers of the other.

'M'mmm, there's nothing to worry about *these* two meaty monsters, although I realise that I'm seeing them at their best before they've taken part in any action,' commented Suzie lewdly, and both men groaned with desire as the gorgeous girl slicked her fists up and down their twitching tools. 'Now I have to tell you that I've been fucked by thicker pricks than these in my time, so it's up to you both to prove that it's not the size of the vessel which matters but how the captain steers his ship.

'Now, who's going to be first?' she asked. Ivor resisted the temptation to say 'I'll toss you for it,' and gasped that Craig could go first as far as he was concerned.

Suzie nodded and let go of his cock as she nimbly straddled Craig's body, one long golden thigh on either side of his hips, poising herself on top of his cock which she still kept grasped in her fist as she ran her free hand between her legs and fondled herself whilst Ivor leaned forward and cupped her soft, heavy breasts in his palms.

She continued to frig herself until she was satisfied that her pussy was ready and, as Suzie's hand emerged from her crack, Ivor noticed that her fingers were liberally coated with her own pussy jism and the pungent aroma filled the air.

'Here we go,' said Suzie as she aimed Craig's bared helmet into the dripping slit of her cunt. 'Just stay completely still, Craig, and let me feel my way round your lovely cock.'

Ivor leaned back and watched the smooth purple knob slide easily inside the pouting pussy lips and Suzie breathed: 'Ooooh, this is going to be so incredibly sexy,' as the first four inches of Craig's cock disappeared inside her and she slid her weight down his rigid pole. She started to slide up and down his stiffstander in little jerks, bouncing herself on his thighs, and with each downstroke she eased more of his shaft inside her.

Craig clasped the trembling girl to him, running his hands up and down her back and squeezing the bouncy cheeks of her backside, as Ivor hauled himself up and positioned himself behind her. Suzie guessed what was on his mind for she panted: 'If you're going to fuck my bum, first smear your dick with some of that sunflower oil from the bottle on the sideboard.'

He was happy to obey this order and when he ran back to stand behind her, his hot, pulsing prick was well-coated with sticky oil, the aroma of which blended well with the smell of sex from the love juices which were now freely flowing from Suzie's pussy.

'Are you ready, Ivor? Slide in gently, I don't often let boys use the tradesmen's entrance,' she declared as she pushed out her beautiful bum cheeks towards him whilst at the same time she slid down to the very root of Craig's thick cock.

It pleased Ivor that Suzie was assuming full command of the situation, because he had no wish to force his shaft into any orifice where it was not wanted, and he achieved the maximum pleasure out of love-making when his partner was also enjoying herself to the full. So he looked lasciviously at her wrinkled little rear dimple that winked at him so invitingly, and then he grasped his greasy shaft in his hand and slid his knob between the crevice of her buttocks. Suzie pushed her bottom back even further and Ivor prised apart her buttocks as he thrust forward, lodging his domed helmet inside her back passage. His vigorous shoves soon gained an entrance for his shaft which was soon well-burrowed deep inside her arsehole.

Suzie gasped out for both Ivor and Craig not to move their trembling tools so she could enjoy the weird, wonderful sensation of being filled with cock from both in front and from behind, and so for a few moments they both stayed still with their erect pricks throbbing against each other with only the thin divisional membrane of her anal canal separating their shafts.

Then, at Suzie's request, Craig started to jerk his hips up and down, his thick tadger sluicing through her engorged cunny whilst she wriggled her bottom in time with the rhythm of Ivor's lusty pecker which was pistoning in and out of her bottom.

She writhed sensuously and cried out wildly: 'Oh yes, yes, y-e-s! God, I've never been so full of prick! It's marvellous! Fuck your cock up my cunt, Craig, whilst Ivor shoots his spunk in my arse! A-a-h-r-e! A-a-h-r-e!'

Suzie screamed with ecstacy as she came with a series of great, all-over spasms which raced through her body, and she was followed only seconds later by the two men who came simultaneously, deluging her arse and cunt with spurts of frothy spunk which ran over the other's balls with every thrust.

Ivor withdrew his deflated shaft from Suzie's backside and he sank onto his knees, mopping his brow whilst Craig flopped back on the sofa. Suzie slid off his thighs and now sat with her long legs stretched wide apart, and she started to stroke her pussy which, like her rear-dimple, had been well-stretched during the wildly unrestrained loveplay.

'Now that's what I call a good fuck,' she commented as she smiled at her two exhausted lovers. 'But neither of your cocks looks able to continue, so it's time to put *Stallion* to the test. Where are the samples that Bennie left for us to try?'

Craig took a deep breath and slowly exhaled before he replied: 'Help yourself, they're in my briefcase on the table.'

Suzie stood up and walked over to the table where she extracted a small black jar from Craig's briefcase. She came back and opened the jar and sniffed the contents. 'Well, at least the stuff smells nice,' she commented brightly. 'So, who's going to be the guinea-pig?'

'Over to you, Ivor,' said Craig as he heaved himself

to his feet and pulled on his underpants. 'I'm afraid that I must love you and leave you as I've just remembered that I promised Cyril Ashberg that I'd call him this afternoon with the results of that survey he commissioned us to carry out on what women think about the new maxi-skirts.'

'Go on, then, we'll let you know how *Stallion* affected Ivor's cock,' said Suzie and she scooped out a dollop of the sticky, orange-coloured cream on the fingertips of her right hand whilst she clamped her left hand round Ivor's shaft and bared the wide helmet by pulling down his foreskin. He groaned and closed his eyes as he surrendered himself to the sensual feel of Suzie's fingers circling around the ridge of his knob and soon his swelling shaft was as rigid as an iron bar.

Craig paused from buttoning up his shirt and remarked: 'So far, so good, Suzie. His prick went on jack almost instantly, but you also have to find out for how long *Stallion* will keep Ivor's cock stiff.'

She looked up at the clock on the wall and said: 'Okay, let's time how long he lasts – it's twenty past three now and I'll check the time as soon as we've finished our fuck.'

'I'll leave you to it, then,' grinned Craig as he slipped on his jacket and said: 'I've got the key of the door and I'll lock it behind me so you won't be disturbed.'

When Ivor heard the lock of the boardroom door click behind Craig he slowly ran his fingers along the length of her body, trailing them lightly over her nipples, along the proud curves of her breasts. He ran them down over her back and she arched slightly as he caught a handful of silky hair at the nape of her neck and wound it round his hand, pulling her head further back as he bent down and kissed her on the lips.

The intensity of her passion startled him as her tongue slashed its way between his teeth, and gently he pushed her back on the sofa and eased her legs apart. His fingers slipped over the dripping lips of her cunt and when he brushed her clitty, Suzie's grip tightened around his cock.

'Let's do *soixante neuf*,' she whispered, and he nodded with a smile as they moved themselves into an arousing new position with Ivor's head buried inside her glossy fleece of pussy hair and Suzie's rich lips pressed against his bulging shaft.

Ivor inhaled the pungent aroma of her moist pussy and he thrust his lips deep inside her cunny, sliding against her erect clitty and sucking it into his mouth as Suzie moaned with delight and, without further ado, brought herself off by rubbing her pussy lips against his mouth and grinding her sopping cunt against his face. Her legs splayed wider as he slurped noisily on her pussy, swallowing her salty love juice as she folded her thighs across Ivor's shoulders and she opened her mouth and washed his knob all over with her tongue. Then Suzie cupped her hands around his tightening ballsack and rubbed her hands lightly along the wrinkled skin as she slowly sucked every inch of his thick shaft down her throat.

A low growl came out from deep inside Ivor's chest as Suzie increased the tempo of her sweet sucking, and when her teeth scraped against the tender cockflesh on the underside of his truncheon, his prick jerked convulsively against the roof of her mouth and she pulled back to let his twitching boner slide out between her lips.

'Fuck me with that big, strong cock,' she murmured throatily and wriggled round onto her back with her knees up and her legs wide apart.

'Yes, ma'am,' replied Ivor softly as he leaned forward and his whole body shook with sexual excitement as the swollen crown of his rock-hard cock teased her cunny lips before he edged his shaft deep inside her juicy love furrow. His hands roved over her jutting breasts, arousing the rosy nipples until they stuck out like two red bullets as he pressed into her until his entire rod was embedded in her creamy snatch.

Ivor began to fuck the quivering girl, slowly at first, but at Suzie's urging he quickly increased the speed of his strokes until his prick slewed in and out of her cunt like a piston and his balls beat a tattoo on the backs of her thighs.

Their bodies slithered against each other as they bucked and heaved whilst the pent-up waves of ecstatic bliss rose to tidal proportions.

'Ram it home, Ivor, I'm almost there,' yelled Suzie, and her fingers raked Ivor's back as she met each of his downward thrusts with upward jerks of her hips, and with one last mighty effort she cried out in ecstasies of pleasure as she achieved her climax and Ivor spouted a stream of hot seed inside her cunt and together they rode the wind . . .

*   *   *

Whilst Ivor and Suzie were testing the efficacy of *Stallion*, his former secretary, Sheena Shackleton, was sitting alone on the side of the small indoor swimming pool that her current employer, the showbiz impresario Bob Mackswell, had constructed inside the basements of the huge Edwardian mansion in Chelsea which he had purchased as soon as Ruff Trayde's first major hit climbed into the American Top Ten charts.

Although Ruff was probably still his biggest earner, Mackswell was also making a small fortune from the several other moneyspinning young pop singers in his stable, and was also engaged in an even more profitable business of property development in three Midlands cities.

Mackswell was an old chum of Martin Reese from their University days, and the tycoon used Cable's services for overall publicity campaigns for Ruff Trayde and, more discreetly, for the Mackswell Organisation's charitable activities – for whilst Mackswell gave generously to a variety of good causes, he confided to Martin Reese that he might as well make sure the right people knew about the donations.

'If the Beatles can get MBEs then I deserve a fucking knighthood,' he had snarled drunkenly at Martin during one of his notorious poolside parties for the famous, and Martin had promised he would bring Mackswell's substantial gifts to the attention of the clutch of establishment personages who were on Cable's payroll as political consultants.

However, Sheena's immediate problem was how to rescue Ruff Trayde's latest record which, as she had explained to Ivor earlier in the day, seemed destined to slide down the charts and would certainly threaten Cable's chances of obtaining a new contract with Mackswell. Her own job, too, might be on the line for she was an ex-Cable employee and had stood up for the agency when it had been suggested that the Organisation might benefit from the appointment of new outside publicists.

The pretty blonde girl sighed, for she enjoyed her work, although she knew she could always find a good secretarial job elsewhere and that Cable would offer her first choice of any vacancies if she wanted to rejoin the agency. I hope Ivor will have some clever ideas for the meeting this evening, Sheena muttered to herself, and then she whirled round as she heard the voice of Chrissie Kingsbridge, Mackswell's private secretary, call out: 'Hiya, Sheena. You okay, love? They say that talking to yourself is the first sign of madness and I wouldn't like to see the men in white coats carrying you out of here in a straitjacket.'

'Hello, Chrissie, oh, it was nothing special – I was just saying that I hope Ivor Belling had something up his sleeve for the crisis conference about Ruff's new record.'

'Or something inside his trousers,' said Chrissie roguishly, slipping out of her bath-robe and stepping down topless into the pool wearing only a pair of the briefest cream bikini bottoms. 'I know you've always burned a candle for Ivor, darling, even though you never went to bed with him when you worked for Cable Publicity.'

'I've never been to bed with him, full stop,' said Sheena severely to the long-legged girl who was lazily swimming across the small pool. 'You know very well that I don't believe in mixing business with pleasure.'

'Well that's not *quite* the case, is it?' giggled Chrissie as she climbed out of the pool. 'Ooh, the water's a bit on the chilly side today. Has Bob turned the heating system off? The mean bugger complained about the size of the electricity bill last week and he's going around switching off lights left, right and centre and I wouldn't be surprised if he's fiddled around with the thermostat to lower the temperature of the water.'

Chrissie sat herself down next to Sheena, who glanced across with a touch of envy as she stared at Chrissie's wet breasts which glistened in the shine of the spotlights. Although Sheena was far from flat-chested, her boobs were not so rounded as Chrissie's magnificent breasts, which reminded Sheena of two snowy white balloons which had been topped with two cute, rosy buttons. She looked down at her own breasts which were pressed inside her black, one-piece swimsuit and squeezed her legs tightly together, saying nothing, but her cheeks coloured up to a pretty pink when Chrissie softly repeated: 'I said that's not quite the case, is it?'

Sheena continued to blush because she knew full well to what Chrissie was referring. Only the other evening both the girls became slightly tipsy after a party to launch the career of Jackie Elstree, one of Bob Mackswell's young hopefuls whose first record was travelling nicely up the charts, and when the guests had left, Chrissie and Sheena were left alone to tidy up.

Sheena could hardly remember who had made the first tentative move which led to the two girls kissing each other in a passionate embrace in the kitchen, and they had climbed upstairs with their arms around each other's waist where they rushed into one of the spare rooms and tumbled into one of the several spare beds. After stripping themselves naked, Sheena had licked and lapped Chrissie's delicious titties and they had diddled each other's pussies before falling asleep in each other's arms.

'Now don't try and tell me that you didn't enjoy yourself on Tuesday night,' said Chrissie, stroking her breasts provocatively which made her crimson nipples stand up into two hard, rubbery corks. 'You kissed my boobs so beautifully when we were in bed together. I'd love you to do so again, darling, and there's no time like the present – we won't be interrupted as everyone else is out this afternoon and we've tons of time before your meeting with Tony Mulliken and Ivor Bigun.'

'His name's Ivor Belling,' said Sheena automatically, but she made no attempt to move Chrissie's fingers when the other girl's hand snaked a path downwards to rest itself between her legs.

'Chrissie, you shouldn't do that,' she added rather belatedly as her friend pulled down the straps of her swimming costume over her shoulder.

'Why not?' demanded Chrissie who now scrambled to her feet and, putting her arms underneath Sheena's shoulders, hauled Sheena to her feet. 'Come on, there's no need for you to be shy,' whispered Chrissie whilst she rolled down Sheena's swimsuit to expose the dimpled plain of her belly.

She was now feeling dizzy with desire as Chrissie kissed her ear and stuck her tongue inside it as her hands roamed freely over her breasts. Sheena knew that the thatch of golden hair over her pussy was becoming moist and she knew perfectly well what was coming next.

'Off with that cozzie,' ordered Chrissie, and Sheena opened her mouth to protest but her lips were quickly covered by Chrissie's and she lifted her bottom to help Chrissie pull down her swimsuit into a damp heap of material around her ankles.

'Open your legs wide now, there's a good girl,' added Chrissie as she knelt down between Sheena's thighs and leaned forward until her nose was just inches from the flaxen fleece which covered her tingling cunt.

'Stop it, Chrissie, you're so naughty,' Sheena murmured but the raven-haired girl's fingers were already at work, spreading Sheena's cunny lips along the length of her crack, with one fingertip delving between them and running all the way from top to bottom before it emerged glistening with love juice.

Sheena's knees trembled as the tiny pink nub of her clitty stood proudly visible between Chrissie's rhythmically moving fingers, and this erotic stimulation pushed her past the point of no return and she panted: 'Oooh, Chrissie, do that again and use your other hand as well.'

'Of course, my love, I do envy you so – you're such a hot-blooded girl with a gorgeous body and I'd love to bring you off with my fingers,' Chrissie replied as she now dipped two fingers of her other hand in and out of Sheena's juicy honeypot. 'My, you're very wet, aren't you?'

'Yes, oh yes! Quicker, please! Another finger! Ohhh!' shrieked Sheena as Chrissie finger-fucked her faster, manipulating her sodden honeypot until a rivulet of love juice spurted out of Sheena's sopping slit and she came in a final, bucking lurch which pitched her on her back, sprawled on the floor while her widespread thighs scissored back and forth in a series of fierce, orgasmic spasms.

Chrissie waited for Sheena to recover from her exciting spend, and then she tugged down her own bikini bottoms and curled herself around Sheena in a *soixante neuf* position with her lips pressed against Sheena's sodden pussy and rubbing her own dark-haired mound against Sheena's mouth.

But just as the two girls began to feast on each other's pubes, Sheena raised her head and said, whispering urgently: 'Chrissie! I heard a noise from outside! Somebody's watching us from behind the door, I'm sure of it.'

'Are you certain?' Chrissie frowned, her lips still busy exploring the delights of Sheena's silky wet muff. 'Then watch me catch the bastard, I hate Peeping Toms!'

She wrapped her arms around Sheena and rolled the pair of them over nearer to the door, and then Chrissie sprung up like a tigress and whipped open the door to expose the horrified figure of Johnny Brennan, the young teenage son of Bob Mackswell's sister, who was working in his uncle's office as an office boy and messenger during the school holidays. He was standing with his flies open and his naked, erect prick clasped in his hand, and it was hardly necessary for the girls to call in Sherlock Holmes to tell them what Johnny had been doing whilst he had been spying upon them!

'Johnny, you naughty boy!' scolded Chrissie, dragging him inside and closing the door behind them. 'How long have you been outside gawping at Sheena and me?'

'Only for a few minutes,' he muttered shamefacedly, his cheeks blushing a fierce shade of red. 'I was looking for Sheena to give her a message from Tony Mulliken to say that he might be a little late for the meeting this afternoon, and as she wasn't in her office I thought I'd look for her in here. Honestly, I didn't mean to pry . . .'

His voice tailed off and Sheena sighed: 'I'm sure he's telling the truth, Chris, let him go and we'll forget all about it.'

'Not so fast,' said Chrissie as she peered downwards at Johnny's penis which had partially shrunk since he had been caught out by the girls, but was still semi-erect and hanging thickly with its wide ruby knob partially uncapped. 'He doesn't deserve to get off scot-free. Darling, come and have a closer look at his John Thomas. What a very big cock he has for a fifteen-year-old boy.'

Johnny gulped as she slid her fingers round his burgeoning chopper and he said nervously: 'Actually, I was sixteen last Thursday.'

'Were you really?' said Chrissie, sliding her fist up

and down his warm, smooth shaft. 'You silly boy, Johnny, why didn't you tell us? We would have given you a nice birthday present, wouldn't we, Sheena? Still, it's not too late, is it? Yes, I'm pretty sure that I can dream up something very suitable to give you – um, on second thoughts, perhaps it's not all that suitable and your Uncle Bob might not approve, but I doubt if you'll be disappointed by what I have in mind.'

She giggled and said: 'Have you ever made love to a girl, Johnny? Be truthful now, don't fib to us.'

The fresh-faced teenager gulped again as he muttered: 'No, never, though my girlfriend and I have got pretty close once or twice.'

'H'mm, I see, well I'm glad you've run a few practice laps but at sixteen, I think it's time for you to take part in a real race and put that nice thick prick to better use than just playing with yourself. Now you would like to fuck me, wouldn't you? And if you're lucky, Sheena might join in and really blow your mind.'

Johnny looked like a bewildered young puppy which had been hotly scolded and then mysteriously stroked, and his eyes lit up as he said breathlessly: 'Oh yes, I should say so!'

'Very well then, but we must do it properly,' said Chrissie as her hands plucked at his shirt. 'The best way to fuck is without any clothes on.'

She unbuckled his belt and pulled his trousers and underpants down to his ankles. 'Stark naked, that's the ticket,' she said encouragingly and when he stepped out of them she took his cock and balls into her hands and kissed him full on his lips.

Then Johnny showed that he may have been an unfledged virgin, but he was no novice in the preliminaries leading up to his heart's great desire. Whilst Chrissie's slippery tongue played inside his mouth and her knowing fingers slid up and down his throbbing shaft, his hands were equally busy, roving from her ripe, rounded breasts to the soft curls around her crotch where her moist pussy lips opened eagerly to his touch.

Chrissie pulled him down to the floor and Sheena watched with fascinated interest as the bi-sexual girl kissed her nipples before straddling the waiting youth and saying: 'Here it comes, Johnny, your very first fuck. Lie back and relax and let me take charge.'

She took hold of his twitching tool which was poking up in salute and placed his knob between her love lips. 'Ready, steady, go!' she cried and slid herself down on his cock until his shaft was completely engulfed inside the clinging wet walls of her love channel.

As soon as he was firmly lodged inside her she swayed back and forth, enjoying to the full the sensuous sensation of riding up and down on his throbbing pole which was now glistening wet from the pussy juice which was trickling out from Chrissie's cunt.

'How do you like that, Johnny?' asked Chrissie as she let out a throaty little laugh. 'Does that feel good or would you prefer me to stop?'

'No, no, please don't stop,' he cried out and Sheena took hold of his hands which had been pressed to the ground and pulled them up to cup Chrissie's breasts. 'Rub her titties, and you'll give her a little extra pleasure,' she kindly explained to Johnny whose hips were now jerking in time with Chrissie's downward plunges upon his excited cock.

Not surprisingly, Johnny was unable to hold on for longer than some thirty seconds before he felt the sperm rising up from his balls and, as they rocked wildly together, the spunk jetted out of his cock in a powerful release as Chrissie slammed herself down on his prick, her cunt clamping him deep inside her as the force of his frothy cum ignited a sweet mini-climax inside her groin.

Later that afternoon, when Ivor listened to Sheena recount how her friend had taken the cherry of Bob Mackswell's nephew, he made a mental note to remind Craig Grey that there was a young age market to be exploited with *Stallion* because teenage youths were often unskilled in the art of waiting for their partners to finish before shooting their loads. Fortunately Chrissie was well aware of this fact and she said lightly: 'Coo, that was a little bit on the quick side,' as she raised herself off Johnny's prick which gleamed wetly as it stood almost as stiff and hard as when she had first sat herself down upon it.

'Still, it's wonderful to be sixteen and able to keep making love for hours and hours,' Chrissie continued whilst she slicked her hand up and down his smooth, blue-veined shaft which immediately swelled back up to its former majestic dimensions.

'Now it's your turn to do some work!' she declared as she lay on her back and pulled his slim, sinewy body over her. His prick slid effortlessly inside her hungry cunny and with barely a pause to take breath, Johnny began to pump up and down in a steady rhythm, his dimpled little bum quivering with every movement of his hips, and this time when he felt like cumming he relaxed and managed to restrain himself so that he could continue to enjoy the wonderful feel of Chrissie's clinging cunny muscles massaging his pulsating prick. She rose to meet him as again and again he rammed home his fleshy rod, and this time it was Chrissie who came first, writhing in the throes of a shuddering orgasm as waves of ecstatic warmth rippled out from her tingling pussy and ran through every fibre in her body.

'Oh Johnny, that was *fantastic*! Now finish off and fill my cunt with jism!' she panted and slid her right hand down between them to squeeze his tight, hairy ballsack. This sent the lad on his way and with one final shove he cried out as his throbbing cock squirted a powerful jet of jism inside her honeypot, filling her to the brim, and the last dribbles oozed out and he sank down on top of her, his weight pinning her to the ground as the last delicious throbs died away. She manoeuvred him over to her side and they lay together, gasping for breath, and Sheena smiled as she saw a blissful smile of fulfilment spread across Johnny Brennan's face.

'So, young man, I'm certain you never expected that particular birthday present,' said Sheena as she idly lifted up his flaccid prick and squeezed it gently before letting it flop back over his thigh. 'I'm not so sure you deserved it, either, though I suppose that Chrissie and I were partly to blame because you had no idea what we were up to when you came looking for me.'

'You did enjoy it, didn't you?' asked Chrissie with

a saucy grin. 'A good fuck is in a different league to a five knuckle shuffle. Now I'd love to continue your education but I must finish some work for your uncle. But if you're a good boy, you can come round to my office at about five o'clock and I'll give you your first lesson in how to eat pussy. It's an art which will help you screw more girls than any of your friends because so few English boys seem to know how to do it. Perhaps they'll get better at it if we join the Common Market!'

By coincidence, a similar thought was crossing the mind of Tony Mulliken, the hard-pressed personal manager of Ruff Trayde, who had been hosting a small reception for a party of continental pop music journalists at his large, well-situated house in Richmond. The normally good-natured pop star had been in a paddy all morning because he had not received a wake-up-darling telephone call from Cliff, his latest boy-friend whose song Ruff had insisted on recording as the A side of his new single against the advice of everyone at the Mackswell Organisation. However, because Ruff had not yet signed his new contract, which would bind him to the Organisation till 1970, not even Bob Mackswell's considerable persuasive powers could induce him to change his mind.

Nevertheless, Ruff was shrewd enough to realise that the good-looking young man who had spent such a passionate night with him after a concert down in Bournemouth, might have used his friendship purely for financial gain. He grimaced when he recalled how

Cliff had borrowed a hundred and fifty pounds from him 'till the royalties from *When Will The Telephone Ring* start rolling in'. Then the camp young man had dropped one or two heavy hints about how he had spent a night with Sheikh Omitochess of Saudi Arabia who had been *so generous* to him and that he had read in the newspaper that the Sheikh was coming to London the following day.

So Ruff had not been in the mood to smile sweetly for the gaggle of French, German and Italian writers whom Tony had invited for a buffet lunch to plug Ruff's new record which had also performed relatively poorly in Europe. Indeed, at first he had refused point-blank to be there until Tony had called in all past favours and begged the unhappy singer to show up. 'It's a unique opportunity to influence these people,' he had cajoled his reluctant star. 'And we're very lucky to find them in London all at the same time. If it weren't for this big charity concert Jake Archer's putting together for Oxfam, I doubt if any of them would have come to London just now.'

Fortunately, Ruff had relented and the press conference had gone ahead without any hitches – indeed, Tony Mulliken had won several plaudits from the continental writers for his fluent French and passable German, and this had undoubtedly made the journalists more receptive to the idea of using the publicity material Tony and Cable Publicity had jointly prepared in their reports.

'I must compliment you, Tony. It's a real pleasure to hear someone like you speaking to me in my own tongue,' said a pretty, petite girl from *Paris-Match*. 'You British are so insular that all foreigners are expected to be able to speak English!'

'Thanks, Manette,' said Tony gratefully as he saw the small fleet of taxis he had booked to take the journalists back to their hotels in Central London draw up outside his front door. 'It's a national failing, I'm afraid, but hopefully we'll get much better at picking up other people's languages once we're inside the Common Market.'

'Your taxis are here, ladies and gentlemen,' he called out and spent the next few minutes standing at the door with Ruff, shaking hands and making his farewells.

'I'll be off, too, Tony,' said the singer and clapped his manager on the back. 'Well done, mate, the record needs all the help it can get and I'm sorry I gave you such a hard time this morning.'

'That's okay. Listen, everyone's entitled to an off-day,' said Tony generously as Ruff's driver opened the door of the Daimler and Tony waved goodbye as the car slowly backed out of the driveway and into the road. He sighed and mopped his brow as he made his way back inside the house, where he slumped down into an armchair and watched the two waitresses busily getting down to the task of clearing up the debris.

But within seconds he was startled to hear a slightly accented, sweet voice behind him say softly in his ear: 'Ah, *ma pauvre* Tony! Are you very tired?'

He looked round and saw that Manette Bergeret had not left with the rest of the group but had chosen to stay behind.

'No, I'm not really tired,' grinned Tony as Manette perched herself on the arm of his chair. 'I just need to recharge my batteries after trying to translate Ruff's answers into French for your colleague Jean-Luc Levoisier from *Le Figaro*. He said he only understood a few words of English, but I think he just wanted me to earn my wages!'

Two dimples appeared at the corners of her mouth as Manette smiled and said: 'It's probably no consolation but you're quite right! Jean-Luc can speak perfect English, but he won't unless he is forced to do so!'

'The miserable bugger,' Tony exclaimed, although he returned Manette's smile and continued: 'You should have told me that you were staying on, Manette. I'm afraid that Ruff's gone home, too, so if you want to speak to him on your own, I'll have to fix up something for tomorrow.'

She shook her head. 'No, that's okay, Tony, I have all I need – I didn't stay to see Ruff. It's just that I have a little time to myself till this evening and unless you have some work to do, I thought we could have a quiet drink together.'

'What a splendid idea!' he said, heaving himself out of the chair. 'Look, I've a decent bottle of bubbly in the fridge. Let's open it.'

'Lovely, I adore good champagne,' she said, slipping into his seat and Tony swept his eyes over the pretty dark-haired girl who had taken off the black jacket of her suit and was sitting down in an expensive white linen blouse through which he could clearly see the swell of her high breasts which were resting in a half cup bra.

Below her blouse Manette was wearing a tight-fitting short skirt and flesh coloured nylon stockings and, as he gazed at her slim, rounded calves, Tony felt his cock begin to swell in the confines of his Y-fronts and he hurried into the kitchen where the two waitresses were about to start on the washing-up.

He fumbled inside his jacket and pulled out a brown envelope from an inside pocket and passed it across to one of the women. 'There you go, Shirley, many thanks to you both for all your help. Just let yourselves out through the back door when you've finished as I've now got to give an interview to a girl from an important French magazine.'

'I'll bet it's *La Vie Parisienne*, Audrey,' said Shirley and the two waitresses started to cackle with glee.

'It's *Paris-Match* actually, you cheeky thing,' said Tony in a tone of dignified reproof as he took out a bottle of vintage champagne from the fridge. 'Now can I have two clean glasses and a tray and I'll get back inside and let Mademoiselle Bergeret carry on with her interview.'

'She'll carry on all right. You'd better keep your hand on your ha'penny, Mr Mulliken,' advised Audrey and the waitresses again dissolved into fits of laughter.

'Ha, ha, very funny I don't think,' said Tony as Shirley gave him a silver tray with the bottle and glasses before opening the door for him. 'Bye bye, Monsewer,' she called after him. 'We'll see you at Mr Mackswell's house next Monday at that party he's giving for that famous American actress, what's her name, Marie Bedford.'

He rolled his eyes skyward and took the tray into the drawing room where Manette was now sexily curled up like a kitten in the chair.

'Stay out of the firing line for I'm not the most skilful opener of fizzy drinks,' warned Tony as he unravelled the silver foil and began to slowly ease off the cork. 'A few months ago I nearly took someone's eye out at Ruff's twenty-second birthday party with a champagne cork, and that was after I'd managed to soak myself with lemonade when I unscrewed a bottle of Seven-Up.'

He pointed the cork at the window but this time there were no problems and it popped out gently onto the tray as the sparkling wine fizzed into the cut-glass tumbler. He filled the second glass and then brought the tray over to Manette and set it down on a side table before giving her one of the glasses and settling himself down at her feet.

'*À votre santé*,' he said, raising his glass, and Manette smiled and replied: 'Cheers, Tony,' and they then proceeded to make substantial inroads into the bottle of what was a very good vintage wine.

By the time they were on their fourth glasses, both Tony and Manette were feeling quite light-headed and they chatted animatedly, until a natural break occurred in the conversation and Tony leaned his head against Manette's legs. He brushed the back of her knees and she said nothing but purred with pleasure when he moved his hand to stroke the inside edge of her right knee.

Tony's heart began to pound as he inched his fingers upwards and Manette moved her legs fractionally apart.

110

He felt the cool, bare flesh above the tops of her stockings and she relaxed and parted her thighs to allow his hand to explore further. He slid his long fingers over her silk panties but when he cupped his hand over her pussy, she pulled herself away from his questing fingertips.

He was about to apologise when Manette stood up and said: 'Tony, I need to freshen up – please, where is the bathroom?'

'It's upstairs, the first room on the right. Here, let me show you,' he replied as he scrambled to his feet. He followed Manette towards the stairs and his pulsing stiffstander pushed uncomfortably against his trousers as he watched the peachy cheeks of her bottom sway from side to side in her tight skirt. She walked slowly up the stairs and almost by accident Tony discovered that by staying back a few steps he could see right up Manette's legs and catch a thrilling glimpse of the garters at the top of her stockings and of her high-cut black panties.

At the top of the stairs she looked down at Tony and gave him a sly smile. 'Where is your bedroom?' she asked and he wordlessly pointed to the white door on his left.

'I'll see you there in five minutes,' she said and then she disappeared into the bathroom. He inhaled deeply and walked purposefully to his bedroom. Once inside, he pulled back the duvet, kicked off his shoes and unknotted his cerise Christian Dior tie which he folded carefully over the back of a chair before lying back on the bed with his head resting against the pillows.

The sultry French girl was as good as her word and a few minutes later she arrived to join him, and immediately Tony noticed that she had taken off her bra and his tongue passed over his upper lip as he looked at Manette's proudly jutting breasts which he could see were now bare underneath her thin, semi-transparent linen blouse.

She sat down next to him, pressing her soft curves against his lean, muscular frame, and when Tony gathered her in his arms, she lifted up her pretty face to be kissed. Their mouths met and in an instant her tongue shot between Tony's lips, probing, lapping and caressing whilst his hands slipped under her blouse at the waist and pushed the wispy material upwards, which momentarily exposed her nude bosoms before he cupped their succulent high-tipped softness in his hands, and his arms trembled as he felt the hardening nipples pushing against his fingertips. There was now a mountainous swelling in his trousers and Manette swiftly wrenched off his belt, unzipped his flies and then assisted Tony to wriggle his trousers over the huge bulge and down to his feet.

Now a sensual crooning noise of anticipation came from Manette's throat as she tugged down Tony's Y-fronts over his hips and freed his thick, pulsing erection which sprung up to salute her.

'*Ma foi*, what a gigantic weapon,' she murmured as she held his swollen shaft tightly in both hands, making it twitch as she worked her hands slowly up and down the fleshy, warm truncheon.

They kissed again and Tony removed one of his hands

to slide it between Manette's thighs. He slid his fingers under her panties and found that she was already very moist and, when he inserted a fingertip between her love lips, her cunt tightened up around his finger when he pushed it in to the first knuckle.

'Oh Tony, I want you to make love to me, but we can't fuck unless you wear *une capote anglaise*, how do you say it in English, a condom,' she said regretfully. 'I am sorry but I cannot take the Pill, it disagrees with me.'

He bit his lip because although he usually carried a packet of Durex in his wallet, he had given his last two condoms to Steve Williams, a member of Ruff's group, The Trayders, after the drummer had been cornered by a sexy young groupie outside the recording studios where the band were laying down backing tracks for Ruff's new LP.

Manette could see the disappointment etched in Tony's face and she sighed and repeated: 'Oh my dear, I am so sorry but you must understand that I cannot take the chance of becoming *enceinte* – however, there are still some other nice games we can play. How would you like to lie back and relax whilst I suck your cock?'

'Sounds like a super idea to me,' he smiled as he lay back and closed his eyes while Manette bent her head to kiss his wide purple knob. He groaned with delight as she swirled her tongue along the underside of his stiff shaft, nibbling at it with her teeth before easing Tony's helmet into her mouth. Sitting back on her knees, she lapped his prick with gusto, lashing her tongue around his pulsing pole and instinctively Tony pressed his hand down upon her tousled head of glossy dark hair as she sucked voluptuously on his thick, twitching tool.

He groaned in ecstasy as wave upon wave of exquisite pleasure radiated out from his groin, and then Manette placed one of her hands under his wrinkled ballsack whilst her head bobbed up and down as she gobbled furiously on his bursting cock, pressing his helmet deeper and deeper inside the warm wetness of her mouth as she gently squeezed his balls.

As he felt himself being drawn inexorably over the precipice, the thought flashed through Tony's mind that he did not know whether Manette would want to swallow his cum. Some girls did and some girls didn't, and he didn't want to upset this gorgeous French filly who had now freed one of her hands so that she could play with her pussy whilst she continued to slurp her tongue up and down Tony's throbbing boner.

'I'm going to spunk,' he warned but, as Manette told him later, she enjoyed the taste of male seed and she simply nodded and began to swallow as, with an immense shudder, Tony's prick expelled a stream of creamy jism which hurtled into her mouth and she gulped down his sticky spend with evident enjoyment. He bucked his hips as Manette sucked his trembling tadger with great skill, coaxing out the last drops of sperm until he had been milked dry, and then she released his fast-deflating shaft from her lips and lifted her head whilst she smacked her lips with satisfaction.

'Well, did you enjoy that?' she asked with a roguish twinkle in her eyes, and Tony nodded and, with a wide smile, he told her sincerely that she had sent him to heaven and back through her magic tonguing of his cock.

'And now you must let me finish you off in the same way,' he declared as he pulled her down beside him. Then the randy couple exchanged a further wet, passionate kiss and, as their tongues twirled together, Tony could taste his own tangy seed inside her mouth.

He settled Manette down on her back and knelt between her parted legs before diving down to kiss the silky black mass of pubic hair which veiled her pouting pussy lips. His hands shot upwards to rub her engorged, rubbery nipples and Tony heard her gasp with pleasure as he buried his face in the moist thatch of her pubic bush and inhaled the delicate cuntal aroma.

'A-a-h! A-a-a-h! A-a-a-a-h!' she breathed sensually as Tony took a firm hold on her rounded bum cheeks and pressed her pussy even closer to his face. He flicked his tongue all around her juicy slit, and Manette whimpered words in French which he could not quite hear as her pussy opened out like a flower, and Tony stuck his tongue between her yielding, pink love lips to probe her stiffening clitty.

Now, whilst Tony teased the full length of her narrow crack with the tip of his tongue, he released his hands from Manette's buttocks and began to finger-fuck the delicious girl, dipping first one, two and then three fingers inside the soft folds of her cunt, and her beautiful body squirmed and writhed as he scraped her erect clitty with his teeth. Then, with his free hand, at first with light strokes and then pressing harder, he rubbed and played with her dripping honeypot, his thumb and two fingers now pressed together as they plunged rhythmically in and out of her tingling cunny, and he swallowed some of the pungent love juice which was now pouring from her sated pussy and let the rest run over his nose and dribble down his chin.

He soaked his lips in her sopping bush as his fingers were drawn even deeper inside Manette's cunt, and he frigged her faster and faster until she exploded into a shattering orgasm, and Tony continued to lick and lap at her quivering cunny lips until the frenzy finally subsided.

'Are you free tonight?' Tony asked softly as they lay quietly in each other's arms. 'Let me take you out to dinner, and then perhaps you could come back here and spend the night with me. By then, I'll be better prepared and we could make love more fully. I can always drive you back to your hotel in the morning.'

Manette kissed his cheek and said: 'It would be wonderful if I could, *ma chere*, but Konrad Kochanski of the *Die Welt* and I have a joint exclusive interview with Monsieur Mick Jagger this evening, and I will have to write up my notes immediately afterwards as my plane leaves early tomorrow and I must file my copy by lunchtime.'

Tony looked crestfallen but Manette suddenly sat up and exclaimed: 'Tony, I have had a brilliant idea. Why don't you come and spend a weekend with me in Paris? You can stay at my apartment and I will show you all the sights of the city.'

'Manette, if I stayed in your apartment we would only go out to eat!' he said as he leaned forward and planted

116

a kiss on each of her nipples. 'But are you serious, because I'd love to come over and see you again. Did you have a date in mind?'

'No, but almost any time is okay with me – how about the weekend after next?' she asked as she reached for her handbag and brought out her diary.

Tony thought for a moment and when he realised that Ruff was spending that weekend quietly with his parents, he replied enthusiastically: 'Yes, that would be super. I'd prefer to drive over. I can get a Friday afternoon ferry crossing if that's okay with you, and if the weather's any good we could go out of town on Sunday.'

'Why not? It all sounds perfectly lovely and my apartment has an underground garage where you can park your car. Here, let me write down my address, 46 Rue General Gewirtz, and my home telephone number is 33–690–251, though you can call me during the day at the *Paris Match* office.'

Tony flipped open the drawer under his bedside table and scrabbled around inside it for one of his business cards. 'Right, and here is my address and telephone number. But as I have to travel a good deal with Ruff, you can always leave a message for me with Sheena Shackleton of the Mackswell Organisation at this number.'

'Okay, that's fine, but write to me, Tony, as soon as you make your travel arrangements so that I will know when to expect you,' she said as she jumped out of bed. '*Mon dieu*! Look at the time! In just over an hour I am supposed to be in Carnaby Street to meet a photographer who is going to take some pictures of Swinging London for me.'

'Don't worry, my love, let's get dressed and I'll give you a lift there,' said Tony as he swung his legs over the side of the bed and he went on: 'No, honestly it's no problem, I must go into town, anyway, because I have to meet some people in Chelsea at half past five. Come to think of it, you'll get there quicker if I drop you at South Kensington tube station and you can take the Piccadilly Line all the way to Oxford Circus.'

They quickly dressed themselves and Tony escorted Manette out of the house and proudly introduced her to his silver Mini Cooper which he had parked outside his garage.

'Have you ever been in a Mini before?' he asked as he started the motor and reversed out of the drive. 'They may not be the most comfortable cars in the world but they're wonderful for dodging in and out of traffic, especially this model which has such a powerful engine.'

'Yes, they're very popular in Paris as they are easy to park as well,' she replied rather nervously as Tony overtook a bus and swerved back a little sharply as another Mini going in the opposite direction suddenly appeared in front of him.

He roundly cursed the driver of the other car and said: 'Sorry if I scared you, but that sod was going far too fast. I'll get you to South Kensington safe and sound, never fear.'

THREE

The Cocktail Hour

'Telling a man that his prick doesn't measure up to expectations is the greatest put-down in the world,' declared Ivor to Craig Grey as the two men sat in Ivor's office swapping thoughts on how best to promote *Stallion*. 'When a girl wants to hurt a guy, making a rude remark about his wedding tackle is the greatest blow she can deliver to his self-esteem.'

Craig nodded in agreement and said thoughtfully: 'True enough, Ivor, there's no doubt that most fellows have little defence against being ridiculed by women and, let's face it, when a man has a sexual relationship with a woman, he is basically leaving himself totally vulnerable, for if his lover isn't impressed by the size of his stiffie, the very symbol of male strength, then his ego will quickly collapse in one fell swoop.'

'I must remember that priceless pearl of wisdom' commented Suzie as she came into the office with some letters for Ivor to sign. 'So, does that mean you really expect girls to bow down and worship our men's mighty cocks every time we make love?'

'No, of course not, you silly thing,' said Ivor with a touch of impatience, 'but you are supposed to be impressed! And that's why for many younger men their penises come in one size only – too small!'

'But naturally that doesn't apply to you guys,' remarked Suzie with a little chuckle, whilst Ivor scribbed his signature on his letters.

'Perhaps it does in some limited, sub-conscious way,' said Craig with a shrug. 'We've all seen dicks which seem much bigger than ours, and however often we're told that most erect organs are usually around the same size, it still crosses your mind that an extra inch or two might come in handy.'

Ivor stroked his chin and said: 'Well, even if you're right, that doesn't help sell *Stallion*. We can't say that rubbing the cream on your old man will make it bigger.'

'No, but surely you can suggest it indirectly,' Suzie ventured as she picked up the correspondence folder. 'After all, if *Stallion* makes your cock hard it *is* increasing its size.'

Ivor looked at his watch. 'I must get going or I'll be late for the crisis meeting with Sheena about Ruff Trayde's new record – but you've made a good point, Suzie, I think we must remember that when we brief Graham to start writing some copy for the first press releases.'

He pulled out his case from under his desk and said: 'Okay, chaps, I'll be at Mackswell's in case of any emergency. We'll firm up some more details about the *Stallion* campaign tomorrow morning.'

Although he had little time in hand, Ivor stopped briefly at the reception desk to speak to Debbie.

'I've had a word with Craig about the situation,' he said quietly, 'and he is genuinely sorry about what happened and will be apologising to you for his behaviour the other evening. According to him, he genuinely misunderstood the situation and, after listening carefully to what he had to say, I'm sure that he's telling the truth.'

Debbie looked up at him and blew him a kiss. 'That's good enough for me,' she said gratefully. 'And I won't make Craig crawl if he realises what he did was wrong. Oh, thank you ever so much, Ivor, it was so kind of you to take such trouble over the pair of us.'

'No trouble, Debbie, I promise you,' Ivor replied somewhat guiltily as he recalled the glorious fuck he had enjoyed with Debbie at the start of the working day.

The sun had finally broken through the clouds and, though the wind still brushed down strongly enough to keep pieces of litter spinning down the road, Ivor found it quite pleasant walking down Holborn as he kept his eyes peeled for a passing taxi. He switched his thoughts away from how to sell *Stallion* to what possible contribution he could make at this forthcoming meeting about giving Ruff Trayde's new record a much-needed hype. There really was little point in flogging a dead horse, Ivor decided as he flagged down a cruising cab, and to call in past favours from journalists, radio producers and disc jockeys would only waste their valuable reserves of goodwill, for *When Will The Telephone Ring?* had been assiduously plugged by all concerned and, if the kids had decided that they weren't that keen on the record, so be it.

'Clayton Street, please. It's off the King's Road, just past Chelsea Town Hall,' instructed Ivor as he climbed into the taxi.

'Right you are, Mr Belling,' said the driver as he switched on the meter, and Ivor's eyes opened wide and he sat bolt upright in his seat. 'How the dickens do you know my – '

The driver let out a guffaw as he stopped in the queue of cars waiting to cross the traffic lights at the busy junction with Southampton Row. Then he turned round and grinned at Ivor and said: 'Hello, Ivor, don't you recognise me? Mind, it's been a good few years since we played football with Nick and Adrian in Aldbourne Park.'

Ivor looked closely at the youngish, balding man and said: 'Blimey, it's Peter Ward, isn't it? How are you, old mate? This is a nice surprise, I thought you'd gone into hotel management somewhere up North.'

'I did, but then I met a girl up in Leeds and we got married a couple of years ago. Well, there's no joy being married to someone working in the hotel business – too many odd hours and having to spend nights away from home – so I packed it in and came back home. My old man's a cabbie, you remember, and he helped me with the knowledge, so it didn't take too long to get my badge.'

'Good for you – and does your wife like London?'

'She loves it! How about you, Ivor, are you still in publicity?' asked his old school friend. 'Here, I don't suppose you would be working for that guy who manages all those pop stars by any chance – what's-his-name now, Bob Mackswell. I had that singer Sally Reynolds in the back of the cab once and I took her to his house in Clayton Street.'

'Yes, as a matter of fact my agency does some work for the Mackswell Organisation,' admitted Ivor, who was then greatly cheered when the cabbie continued: 'Then could you get me Ruff Trayde's autograph, please? My young sister is crazy about him. She buys all his records, even the last one which she didn't like all that much.'

That settles it, thought Ivor grimly. We let Ruff's current disc sink or swim and concentrate on making sure that the next song he records is a fucking sight better than *When Will The Telephone Ring*?

'Of course I will, Pete, scribble down her name and address when we get to Clayton Street and I'll ask Ruff to send her a personally signed photograph.'

The lights changed to green and Peter Ward turned back and gunned down his accelerator to get in front of a line of lumbering buses. 'Thanks very much, Ivor, you're a scholar and a gentleman,' he called back as he manoeuvred the taxi into a clear lane and sped on his way to Cambridge Circus where they were forced to stop, even though the lights were green, as a large lorry heading north up Charing Cross Road had blocked the junction and none of the traffic could move across into Northumberland Avenue.

Peter Ward roundly cursed the selfishness of the errant lorry driver and Ivor caught the last few words of his tirade when he moved across to the small seats by the window which separates the driver and his passengers in London taxis.

'Nothing you can do, Pete, it won't be your fault if I don't get there by half past five,' said Ivor soothingly. 'It must be nerve-wracking to drive a taxi in London these days.'

'You can say that again! Let's face it, everyone who gets into the cab is in a hurry – or otherwise they'd take a bus or even walk! What's worse is when people have a train to catch or if they're late for the theatre, and you're to blame if you can't get them there on time.'

'I can understand their frustration, but you just can't jump over the traffic,' he groaned as the lights turned red just as the lorry finally moved on and unblocked the junction.

'Still, you must occasionally get some characters in the cab,' said Ivor and Peter Ward laughed and said: 'Now and then, though more often you get nutters at two o'clock in the morning. Actually, I haven't had any really famous people in the cab, but the other week I worked a couple of nights which can be hard graft, but it makes a nice change not to be stuck in all the jams. Well, at about eleven-thirty I picked up a couple outside Broadcasting House and was told to drive to a posh block of flats in Highgate. I thought I recognised the girl from the telly although I couldn't remember her name, but the older chap she was with didn't look like an actor and I had no idea who he was.'

The traffic inched forward and Ivor kept his ear to the partition in the window as Peter Ward went on: 'I soon found out, though! The girl cuddled herself next to this chap and soon they're necking away like crazy.'

'I thought the driving mirror in taxis was specially positioned so that you couldn't see what was going on in the back seat,' Ivor said with some concern, for he had been partially undressed in a taxi only a couple of months before by two girls from the Hunkiedorie after a wild private party thrown for a select band of his best customers by Nedis Decopoulos, the suave Cypriot who owned the Club.

'Don't you believe it! Anyhow, I hadn't shut the glass panel so I could hear every word they were saying. It turned out that this arty-looking chap was a radio producer and he was complimenting the girl on her performance in the play which had just been broadcast on the Home Service.

'"Flick, you sounded so wonderfully sexy in that love scene with Roger," he said to her. "Whilst you were speaking I closed my eyes and started to fantasise about how I'd like to make love to you myself."

'She wriggled as he slid his hands inside her coat and said: "Oh Jeremy, you are such a flatterer, I wasn't *that* good!"

'"Yes you were, my poppet," he insisted and I saw him slide a hand across her knee. "When you were telling Roger how much you cared for him, I started to imagine myself lying naked on the bed with my cock standing to attention and you kneeling between my thighs wearing nothing but a skimpy pair of panties. I had to hide my erection from the other people in the control room as I thought about how I would pull down your knickers and look at the silky bush which covers your mouth-watering little crack. Oh, how I would lovingly finger your darling wet pussy until you lowered your head and began working your lips up and down the shaft of my rock-hard prick whilst you cupped my balls in your hands – and then I would turn you over and fuck you from behind and we'd both come in torrents!"

"'Gosh, that sounds exciting," she said to him, and I noticed that naughty old Jeremy had moved his hand under her skirt and was tickling Flick's pussy with his fingers!

"'Fantasy's fine but reality is even better," he said and he pulled her face towards him and they began kissing so passionately that I could hardly concentrate on the road! He soon had his hand inside her coat and was fondling her breasts, and she unzipped his flies and pulled out one of the biggest boners I've ever seen. I tell you, Ivor, remember the Thick Prick Club which we belonged to at school? If dimensions counted when it came to elect the president, this geezer would have been returned unopposed as no-one could have stood against him!'

Ivor laughed out loud and remarked: 'Christ, what would have happened if a police motorcyclist had pulled up next to you at traffic lights?'

The driver shuddered and said: 'Ivor, it doesn't bear thinking about! Although I was only driving the cab, you'd be surprised what the Public Carriage Office can throw at us if a taxi driver's involved in something which isn't kosher! Licensed black taxis are strictly regulated, you know, not like those fucking fly-by-night minicabs.

At best I would have had to give evidence in court, and can you imagine what a field-day my friends would have had if the case had got into the papers!'

'Well, it's as well they didn't get caught,' chuckled Ivor, holding on to the strap on the side of the cab as they swung into Piccadilly. 'What did these lovebirds do next?'

'She gave Jeremy a hand-job whilst he unbuttoned her blouse and unhooked her bra. "Be a darling and stuff it in my bag," she told him, which he did before he started to play with her tits.

'We were now almost at Tufnell Park and I hoped she'd finish him off by the time we got up to the top of Highgate Hill. I took a quick look at them as I reached Archway and she was pummelling his prick so violently I thought she was going to pull it off. Then he cried out and I saw a huge jet of goo shoot out of his cock. I just hoped that it would all land on his trousers – I always keep a bottle of stain remover in the cab, but I didn't much fancy having to clean his cum off the seat.'

'I dropped them off at Cholmondley Gardens and I must say that Jeremy gave me a bloody good tip! Luckily, the seat wasn't stained so all was well and I drove on to the cab shelter and had a cup of tea and a bloody good laugh with some of the boys about it all before I finished my shift.'

Peter ended his story as they reached Sloane Square and a few minutes later he pulled up outside Bob Mackswell's imposing house in Clayton Street.

Ivor gave his old chum a generous tip and said: 'Don't forget to give me the name and address of your sister, and Ruff will send on a signed photograph.'

'Blimey, I nearly forgot. Here, I'll write it down on a piece of paper,' said Peter gratefully. 'Thanks again, Ivor, nice to see you again.'

'All the best, mate, look after yourself,' he called out as Peter turned the taxi round and picked up a woman who was standing on the other side of the road.

Ivor smiled ruefully as he considered the vagaries of fate which had left him footloose and fancy free on a salary of five thousand pounds a year which was almost a thousand pounds more than the average family doctor – whilst poor old Peter Ward, who had been consistently top of Ivor's class at school, was probably having to work a six day week to make half that amount.

'Must be the luck of the draw,' Ivor muttered as he pressed the bell of the answerphone at the aptly numbered 69 Clayton Street. He waited and, not receiving any answer, he pressed the button again and this time Sheena's voice came through and asked who was calling.

'Hi, Sheena sweetheart, it's me, Ivor,' he said into the grille, and when he heard the electronic buzz he pushed open the door which shut smartly behind him as he walked through the hall, straight through into Sheena's office.

'Answering the door yourself now?' he queried as he exchanged a friendly peck on the cheek with his former secretary. 'Everyone else on strike or has Bob sacked all the workers?'

'Jason and Matthew are with His Highness in

Manchester for the opening of that new play for which Bob's put up the money,' answered Sheena as she waved Ivor to take a seat. 'And everyone else, except for Chrissie who's upstairs in Bob's quarters, is either out or gone home. And I'm afraid that Tony Mulliken called earlier to say he may be a wee bit late, so I hope you didn't rush to get here so promptly.

'Damn, I really want to get away pretty smartish this evening,' grumbled Ivor irritably. 'There'll be hell to pay if I don't pick up my girlfriend at half past seven.'

'I would think we'll be able to wrap everything up in an hour or so. Would you like a drink whilst we wait for Tony? I can offer you Scotch, white wine or beer, or will you join me for some lovely fresh Jaffa orange juice?'

'I'll have the same as you, please,' he replied, and Sheena pulled out a jug of orange juice from the small fridge in the corner of her office.

'Tony shouldn't be too late. He's probably just seeing to one or two bits and pieces after Ruff's press conference for European journalists,' said Sheena consolingly as she poured the juice out into two glasses and passed one to Ivor. 'You'll like this juice, Ivor, it's very refreshing.'

Ivor took a long sip from his glass and gave her a nod of appreciation. 'It is nice, isn't it? Funnily enough I signed up a new client from Israel today but he's selling something very different from orange juice.'

He told her about Bennie Hynek's plan to market *Stallion* erection cream in Britain and Sheena burst out into a fit of giggles. 'This just confirms what I've always believed – men are really ruled by their pricks!

God, why do you men always feel this terrible necessity to perform? It's all to do with power and success, isn't it?'

'Maybe so,' Ivor conceded with a smile. 'But on the other hand, as women have become sexually and socially liberated by the Pill, there's more pressure on guys to give great performances in bed even if we're tense, uncertain or even a little scared.'

'Well, good luck with your new client, Ivor. I suppose that if *Stallion* does nothing else, it could help lads who are nursing their wounded pride after having suffered cruel comments about their cocks from dissatisfied partners and give them back their confidence.'

The entryphone telephone buzzed and Sheena added: 'Ah, with a bit of luck this might be Tony Mulliken.' She picked up the receiver and gave Ivor the thumbs-up sign. 'Hiya, Tony, so you made it on time after all. Come on in.'

Ivor sat down to open his case and take out the Ruff Trayde file. 'Pour out an orange juice for Tony, he deserves it,' he said with relief, for he was genuinely concerned that if he broke his date that evening, Mandy might well carry out her threat to ditch him. Despite working in a similar field, she did not appreciate that someone in Ivor's position could not always bring down the shutters smartly at six o'clock like the local greengrocer.

There was a beaming smile on Tony Mulliken's face when he stepped into the office, which was hardly surprising for only a few minutes ago he had exchanged a final passionate kiss with Manette before he had dropped her at South Kensington Underground station, and he could look forward to a saucy weekend in Paris with the deliciously sexy French girl.

He accepted the offer of an orange juice from Sheena and, as he slipped off his jacket and hung it over the back of a chair, Ivor asked him if the lunch-time press conference had been successful.

'It went off like a dream,' said Tony with enthusiasm. 'We had nine journalists from France, Italy and West Germany and Ruff was his usual charming self and answered all the questions very professionally. Of course, I can't guarantee what's going to appear in the press, but I'm certain we'll have a wonderful write-up in *Paris-Match*.'

'Thank goodness for small mercies,' Sheena remarked whilst she flipped open her notebook, tapped her Biro on the desk and said briskly: 'Look, you both know why we're having this meeting. Bob's very unhappy about the reception we've had for Ruff's new single, and he wants us to come up with some new ideas to give the record a fresh hype. So is there anything else we haven't tried? Ivor, what's your view?'

'Frankly, in my opinion we shouldn't do anything at all,' said Ivor bluntly. 'Now I hate to sound defeatist, but the simple truth of the matter is that *When Will The Telephone Ring?* was never a strong enough record to make the Top Ten. It was only Ruff's name which managed to get the record into the charts in the first place. Remember how even Bob begged Ruff to make the song a B side, but that little squirt who wrote the fucking song wouldn't hear of it.'

He continued by telling Tony and Sheena of the conversation he'd had with the taxi driver who had brought him to Clayton Street, which proved that not even the most devoted of Ruff's fans were that keen on the record. 'In any case, it might not be such a bad thing if the record didn't do so well as the previous singles,' he continued emphatically. 'For a start, it would teach Ruff a valuable lesson and he wouldn't be tempted to mix business with pleasure again by letting his boyfriends get involved with his music. 'As soon as possible we must commission a top team like Louis Baum and Fred Newman to write Ruff's next single and get someone like Harry Barr to produce it. Then we release the record as quickly as we can and hey presto, everyone will have forgotten about *When Will The Telephone Ring*?'

Sheena jotted down some notes and looked directly at Ivor and said: 'I'm not saying you don't have a case, but I wonder how Bob will react if I put that argument to him. He might say that you're not working hard enough for your fees.'

Tony held up a hand. 'Well, for what it's worth, I agree with Ivor. There's no point throwing good money after bad,' he said firmly. 'The only way we'll ever get any more radio plays is to pay the pirates to plug the record and, to be honest, I don't think even another *Top Of The Pops* will do much good. Bob's no fool, Sheena. If we tell him straight we don't think it's worth trying to hype *When Will The Telephone Ring*?, I think he'd listen to us.'

There was silence for a moment and then Sheena

heaved a heavy sigh and unlocked a drawer in her desk. 'I'd hoped I wouldn't have had to mention this, but now I'll have to explain why we can't sit on our hands as far as this rotten record is concerned.'

She took an envelope out of the drawer and passed it across to Ivor. 'Tony, perhaps you could read this charming epistle addressed to Cliff Pendlebury over Ivor's shoulder,' she said bleakly, and she sat back in her chair to wait until the two men had scanned the handwritten letter which they immediately noticed was in Ruff's own handwriting.

'Cliff Pendlebury?' echoed Tony with a grimace. 'I have a horrible suspicion that this missive isn't going to be some light holiday reading.'

They read the letter carefully from the beginning . . .

Darling Cliff,

How super it was to meet you after the concert on Saturday night. It was very nice of you to tell me how much you liked my act, and even nicer of you to invite me back to your place for an intimate little fancy-dress party.

Didn't we get legless, though! I don't think your young friend Wayne knew where he was when he pulled down his tennis shorts and started jacking off, but it was great fun watching his shaft get hard and then seeing his spunk shoot out of his big cock. But what was a bigger turn-on was when you asked me to leave the rest of the guests and go upstairs with you into your bedroom.

I simply adored the way you pretended to resist

when I began to undress you, and my own prick was as stiff as a board when I pulled down your pants and revealed your round little bum cheeks and your rock-hard, circumcised cock. Remember how we both flung off the rest of our clothes and you grabbed my shaft and began to lick and suck my uncapped knob?

Honestly, Cliff, I felt sensations I never knew existed when you took my balls in your mouth whilst you jerked me off, and we rolled onto the bed and you tossed me off so beautifully and I came like a volcano and shot my wad onto your flat, muscular stomach.

Since then we have savoured each other's bodies like fine liqueurs many times and, though we cannot be together again until I finish this wretched Midlands tour, I want you to know that your incredibly beautiful penis has become the most important thing in my life.

All my love,
Ruff

Tony covered his head with his hands and moaned aloud. 'How did you get this letter, Sheena? My God, it's pure dynamite. If anyone from the press ever got a peep, poor old Ruff would be done for. And if the pair of them have been fiddling around with young Wayne, who's probably under twenty-one, he can also look forward to a visit from P.C. Plod!'

'Yes, old mate, but there's a more immediate problem to hand,' said Ivor promptly. 'This isn't the original letter but only a photocopy, and it's my guess that

Cliff sent Sheena and Bob copies after stressing how important it was to keep plugging *When Will The Telephone Ring*? because I'm assuming that Cliff is the guy who wrote the crappy song.'

'Top of the class, Ivor,' said Sheena with a trace of bitterness in her voice. 'Bob went bananas when he received his copy of Ruff's letter and asked Irving Gottlieb, his solicitor, for his advice. But Irving warned him about contacting the police because Cliff has only hinted at how he wants more effort put into marketing the record in telephone calls, and he can always deny having sent us photocopies of that letter. He might even try to say that we stole it from him and were blackmailing him! So we're caught between a rock and a hard place, boys, and not even Bob is sure how we deal with Mr Pendlebury.'

They sat in silence for some thirty seconds and then Tony said slowly: 'How about putting the frighteners on the little wanker? I know a couple of tasty fellows who could do the job. On first sight, you wouldn't like to meet Grahame or Sean on a dark night, though in actual fact they are very professional gentlemen who rarely have to lay a finger on anyone. However, they are very good at making people fully aware that if they don't start to toe the line, the consequences could be very painful.'

'Hey, that's a bit over-the-top, isn't it?' said Sheena, but Ivor was all in favour of the suggestion. 'You have to fight fire with fire, and blackmailers deserve everything that gets thrown at them,' Ivor said as he turned to Tony and asked: 'Are these two guys trustworthy?'

'Safe as the Bank of England, and much more so than the average London nick which only needs one bright spark to tip off the *Daily Mirror* for all hell to break loose,' he replied with a grin.

'Okay then, you've convinced me,' said Sheena decisively. 'I must contact Bob first thing tomorrow morning and inform him what our street-wise consultants recommend. Tony, I'll call you if he gives us the go-ahead.'

'Don't write anything down, Sheena,' advised Tony as he snapped shut his folder. 'And you'd better tell Bob that Grahame and Sean don't come cheap, though in the long run they'll be a lot less expensive than buying airtime on the pirate stations.'

'And there's something else to consider. If we don't scare off Cliff now, he'll soon be making further demands like writing another song for Ruff or grabbing the publishing rights to the B side,' declared Ivor firmly.

Tony smiled and said: 'Mention that to Bob, love, and I'll bet folding money that he'll be all in favour of sending round the heavy mob *toute de suite*. You do realise that Mr Mackswell makes a small fortune out of publishing those B sides himself, don't you?'

'I never knew that,' admitted Sheena. 'I thought that Austin and Webb was just another music publisher.'

'You astonish me, Sheena,' exclaimed Ivor in surprise. 'Why, even I knew that particular company is fully owned by Bob, and every time a record is sold he makes a nice few pennies in royalties.'

Sheena digested this information and said: 'I suppose

I should have guessed why Austin and Webb were given the B side rights on all Ruff's records and on most of the singles put out by Bob's other artistes. Actually, I thought we often gave the B side rights to producers and disc jockeys as thank-you gifts for services rendered.'

'Hush your mouth, girl! As if we'd ever stoop so low!' said Tony with a wicked smile. 'Next you'll be accusing us of sending out gophers to buy up records at the shops which supply data for the charts!'

'Oh, that's old news. I've known all about that scam from the first week I worked here. But what exactly is a gopher?'

'Very simple, my sweet. A gopher is an odd job person, some one at the beck and call of the stars or the directors and goes for this, goes for that, sandwiches, drinks or whatever,' Tony explained and he added: 'Well, that just about wraps it up, children, and I'll be on my merry way back to Richmond. Call me after you've spoken to His Lordship, Sheena love, and I'll get my lads on the job. By the bye, does Ruff know that the love of his life is putting the squeeze on us? If not, don't you think he should be told?'

'Bob says we should resolve the problem before talking to Ruff as it will only upset him and Bob wants to get the new contract under his belt,' said Sheena as she rose from her seat. 'Okay, chaps, thanks for a short but profitable meeting.'

Ivor glanced at his watch and was happy to see that he had time to kill before his *rendezvous* with Mandy at half past seven.

'Are you going home now?' he asked Sheena.

'Or have you time for a drink before you call it a day?'

She thought for a moment and then decided not to take up his offer. 'Can I take a rain check on the drink, Ivor? As we've finished the meeting early, I'd like to get back home and do some chores. I've a pile of ironing to do and I'd also like to wash my hair tonight. Tell you what, though, Chrissie Kingsbridge is still upstairs and I'm sure she'd be delighted to join you for a quick drink. And whilst you're there, could you please tell her I've left and that she should lock up.'

'Okay, I'll pop upstairs and ask her, and perhaps we'll have that drink next week. What would be even better is if you came round to Holborn one day and let me take you out for lunch.'

'Thanks, Ivor, I'll give you a ring. Enjoy the film tonight,' she said as he waved goodbye and walked up the flight of stairs to Chrissie Kingsbridge's office. He knocked on the half-open door and walked in to see the pretty girl holding a huge black vibrator in her hand whilst she was poring over a copy of *Ram*, one of the more explicit American magazines which was banned in Britain, though smuggled copies did circulate in London amongst the select circle of the swinging showbusiness set.

Chrissie looked up and said without any embarrassment: 'Hi there, Ivor, your conference with Sheena finished already? I bet you wish that you could wrap up all the meetings so quickly.

'And I bet you also wish you had something like this dangling between your legs as well!' she added impudently, holding up the thick ten-inch-long dildo for Ivor's closer inspection.

He peered at the plastic vibrator which was textured like a giant penis and shook his head. 'No, not really – why should I settle for something smaller than the cock with which I've naturally been blessed!' he observed, and Chrissie let out a throaty chuckle as she smoothed her fingers along the shaft of her sex toy.

'You must prove that to me some time,' she said with a saucy glint in her eyes. 'Meanwhile, I feel like trying out this monster. It's called "The Black Mamba" and as it says in *Ram*: "Here's the most amazing pussy pleaser ever produced! The mere sight of this marvellous monument of manhood will start the jungle rhythms beating inside the sticky moistness of any hot-blooded girl's snatch! She'll be soothed and grooved with this tower of power, a space-age machine which vibrates, thrusts and probes every nook and cranny of her cunt."

'I think I'll give it a try tonight, unless there's anything better you can suggest,' she said suggestively.

'I'm afraid I have to get back to the office for an important conflab with Martin Reese,' fibbed Ivor, who was loath to look a gift horse in the mouth. 'But I do have time for a quick drink before I go. Tony and Sheena have left and she's asked you to lock up, by the way, but I'd be delighted if you'd join me for a glass of something.'

'Sure, why not?' said Chrissie, putting the Black Mamba and her magazine away in a drawer. 'Let's go down and help ourselves to a bottle of Bob's white wine from the fridge.'

She switched off the lights and went downstairs, and they settled themselves down back in Sheena's office. Ivor, who disliked waste, opened a half bottle of Frascati he found at the back of the fridge and poured out glasses of the refreshing, chilled wine for them.

They chatted about Bob Mackswell and Ruff Trayde and, although Ivor said nothing about the latest problem regarding the singer, Chrissie said: 'Of course I know that Ruff's a woofter. Well, he thinks he is but I'm not so sure he couldn't switch to the mainstream if he were given a chance. I mean, there's a little bit of bi-sexuality in us all, don't you think?'

'I'm not so sure about that,' said Ivor guardedly, 'because I promise you that the idea of going to bed with another guy is in no way a turn-on as far as I'm concerned. What consenting adults do to each other is their own affair but I'm strictly a girls-only guy.'

'Maybe you are, Ivor,' Chrissie said earnestly. 'I don't mean to question your masculinity, but personally I like to try out everything once and between you and me, I enjoy making love to another girl occasionally. Oh, I wouldn't want to screw with other girls all the time but, as a change from a cock now and then, I don't mind admitting that I find a little lesbian lovemaking very nice.'

Ivor shrugged his shoulders and remarked: 'That's fair enough. As the Yanks say, different strokes for different folks.'

She smiled and held out her glass for a refill. 'Oh,

don't get me wrong, I love a hot, thick cock in my cunny as much as the next girl. Why, only this afternoon I fucked Bob's nephew, young Johnny Brennan, and I had a great time at a party last night with two of the boys from Ruff's band.'

'I'll lay odds that one of them was Steve Williams,' grunted Ivor as he downed the rest of his wine. 'One of these days his cock will fall off if there's any justice left in the world.'

Chrissie giggled and said: 'Perhaps, though it was in good enough working order last night! If anyone disgraced themselves, it was me. I went upstairs with Steve and Roger Dyotte, the bass guitarist, and we locked ourselves in one of the bedrooms. They sat me on the dressing-room table and undid my blouse and bra whilst they stripped off all their clothes except for their pants. Now, did you know that Steve has a history degree? Well, I learned something from him last night because the cheeky monkey kissed my nipples and said: "Chrissie, you have the most gorgeous titties and they're so nice and firm. Now, did you know that in the Middle Ages, girls rouged their breasts?" and before I could say anything he dipped a brush into a pot of rouge and began smearing it all over my bosoms. Actually he did quite a good job and then he finished off by putting lipstick on my tits.

'Then he and Roger began licking it off, which made my nipples harden up whilst they finished undressing me, taking turns to finger-fuck my pussy whilst I pulled down their pants and began wanking them off.

'So there I was with Roger's stiff boner in one

hand and Steve's even thicker big cock in the other. I pulled them by their dicks over to the bed and we lay down on the eiderdown and I teased them by running their cocks around the outside of my crack without actually putting their knobs inside my cunny lips. Then I played with their pricks in my mouth and sucked each of them off. Roger lost control and spunked all over my breasts, but then Steve rolled me over onto my tummy, pulled up my hips and, after parting my bum cheeks, proceeded to give me the most wonderful hard fucking from behind whilst Roger stuck his head under my pussy and nibbled my clitty.'

'Sounds as though a good time was had by all,' quipped Ivor as he put down his glass and reluctantly tore his eyes off the sensuous girl who was unashamedly pouting her lips at him. 'Chrissie, I must be off now, but why don't we make a date for dinner one evening next week? I don't have my diary with me but I'll give you a ring tomorrow morning and perhaps we can fix something up.'

'Okay, Ivor, I'll look forward to hearing from you, if only because I want to see if you really can match up to The Black Mamba!' she laughed and blew him a kiss as she added: 'Off you go now, we mustn't keep Martin waiting!'

Ivor hurried out of the building and walked down the King's Road towards Sloane Square. There were few taxis to be seen in the evening rush-hour traffic and all of them were already occupied. All the passing buses were full up with office workers returning home or going further into town for the evening, so he decided to trudge down towards the nearest Underground station. I'll have to travel down the bloody tube, he muttered to himself, but consoled himself with the thought that he would easily make it in time to meet Mandy at her office.

However, just as he quickened his pace to cross a road junction, a black taxi squealed to a halt beside him. He looked up and to his great delight saw that the driver was none other than Peter Ward who had turned off his taximeter, although there were no passengers in the back of the cab.

'Blimey, Ivor, I don't see you for years and then twice in one afternoon!' called out the driver. 'Where do you want to go? I've finished my shift and I'm on my way home but I'll drop you off somewhere if you're not too far out of my way.'

'I need to get back to Holborn – Theobald Street to be exact,' said Ivor hopefully and, to his joy, Peter told him to hop in. 'Couldn't be better, Ivor, I'll take you all the way because Wendy and I live in Gants Hill, so I'll have to pass by your front door. Where are you living these days?'

'Oh, I've a bachelor flat up in Hampstead,' said Ivor as he gratefully climbed into the cab and took up his previous position, sitting behind Peter with his mouth pressed to the partition in the glass separating the driver from his passengers.

'Hampstead? Well, there's another coincidence,' said Peter Ward, turning his head as he stopped the taxi at a red light. 'You'll never believe it, but did you notice that after I dropped you I picked up a girl on the other side of the road?'

'Yes, but I only caught a glimpse of her,' Ivor said vaguely. 'Wasn't she wearing a blue dress? And I thought I noticed she had a large case beside her on the pavement.'

'Right on both counts. What a cracker she was, too. A nice big girl in her late twenties with a lovely pair of knockers which she must of been proud of 'cos the neckline of her dress was so low that when she bent down to pick up the case, I could almost see what she had for breakfast!

'Anyway, she climbs in and tells me to go to Gordon Avenue in Putney and when I drop her at this posh house, naturally I got out and opened the door for her. "Here, let me carry that case for you," I said and I brought it up to the front door.'

'Carry on, Peter,' urged Ivor, craning his neck to hear the rest of his old friend's anecdote as Peter swung in front of a slow-moving Morris Oxford whose driver shouted out a coarse comment upon the legitimacy of Peter Ward's birth.

The taxi-driver leaned out of the window and bellowed back: 'And fuck you too, dog-breath!' before pressing his head back against the glass and saying to Ivor: 'Where was I? Oh yes, I dumped the case down whilst she opened the front door and then I heaved it inside and put it on the floor whilst she started scrabbling in her handbag for her purse.

'Then she looked up at me and said: "Oh dear, how embarrassing! I've just come back from Paris and I don't seem to have any money on me at all except a fifty franc note. I'm sorry, would you write your name and address down on a piece of paper and I'll send you a cheque when my husband comes home tomorrow morning."

'Now, like all cabbies, I've been bilked for the fare a few times, but I had a gut feeling that this was no take-on. I said: "Look, it's hardly worth sending me a cheque for eight bob. I'll gladly call it quits in exchange for a nice cup of tea."

'Her face brightened up and she said: "Do you mean that? I could just do with a cuppa myself. Come on into the kitchen and I'll put on the kettle."

'Well, we got talking and she told me her name was Barbara and that she was a fashion designer for Marcus and Nathan's in Bond Street. "So you travel a fair amount then? Nice work if you can get it," I remarked but she said: "Not really, when I'm in Paris or Rome all I ever see are the main shopping areas and the inside of a few posh shops."

'"Yes, I suppose so, and I imagine you miss your husband in those lonely hotel rooms," I said rather forwardly, but thankfully she didn't take offence. No, indeed, far from it. She winked at me and said: "Alan's away so much these days on business I hardly see him, and even when he is here he's so exhausted I might as well be on my own at nights."

'Ay, ay, I'm in with a chance here, I thought, but I never quite know how serious women are when they give you the old come-on.'

Ivor grunted his agreement and commented: 'There's only one way to find out, Pete – make the next move and see if you get any reaction. On the other hand, you have to be prepared for any response from a French kiss to a swift knee in the nuts!'

'Very true, only this time it looked like I was standing on the penalty spot with the goalie on the ground, and I had all the time in the world to put the ball in the net! The crunch came almost immediately when Barbara opened the larder door and said: "Peter, would you be kind enough to reach up for the packet of tea-bags on the top shelf?"

'"Of course," I replied and as I reached up I pressed against her, taking care to brush the front of my trousers against her bum. For a split second I thought I might have missed the open goal, but then she pushed her backside firmly against my cock which was already stiff. I slipped my hands over her lovely big breasts and gave them a friendly squeeze whilst she rubbed her buttocks against my flies.

'Then she turned round and, hey presto, we were in a clinch. We were locked together in one of those wet, slobbery kisses as Barbara pulled me inside to the drawing room where she helped me unbutton the top of her dress and unhook her bra. But when I started rubbing her big brown nipples between my fingers she went into a really wild frenzy. She slid down on her knees with her massive, swinging breasts pillowing against my knees as she unzipped my flies and pulled out my cock. The next thing I know is that my trousers and pants are on the floor and she's giving me the most fabulous blow-job, tonguing all round my knob and sucking my shaft inside her mouth, slurping all the way down to my hair whilst she's sliding her hand up and down it.

'I could feel the pressure building up in my balls, and then she pulled her head away but kept her hand going whilst she slid my dick tight in between her big breats, which she pulled together, and this was more than I could take. "Go on, big boy, fuck my tits," she cried out and with one jerk I came and squirted my cum all over her jugs till it was dripping down onto her tummy. Barbara got off as well, closing her eyes and massaging my sticky jism into her breasts, rubbing her palms in slow circles across her hard, stiff nipples.'

'Peter, it sounds as though you did better than if she'd have had the eight bob she owed you in her handbag,' remarked Ivor with a grin, and the driver gave a short laugh and replied: 'Hold on a minute, that gobble might have taken care of my eight bob, but what about a tip?'

'M'mm, I'm sure Barbara wasn't a, what do you cabbies call passengers who don't tip, a "legal"?'

'She sure wasn't! Whilst I was still recovering, Barbara lay back on the carpet, purring softly, still kneading and squeezing those beautiful big breasts. Then she wrapped her arms around my hips and pulled me down next to her. "Help me take off my dress, it's a Christian Dior and I mustn't get it marked," she said, and when she'd wiggled out of it I laid it down carefully on a chair. Then she rolled down her panties and I was unbuttoning my shirt when she opened her legs and showed me her glistening red crack and hissed: "Don't worry about that, I'm ready for you!"

'She grabbed hold of my prick and gave it a few quick wanks until my shaft stiffened up again, and then I rubbed my knob against her pussy and buried my tool in her sopping snatch.

'"Go on, Pete, make it hard and fast – I need a good fuck and I want to feel every inch of your thick, fat cock inside my pussy!" she gasped and clamped her feet round my back, drumming her heels against my spine whilst I pounded away in and out of her juicy honeypot. Then she got on top and started doing all the business as she rode me, tossing her head this way and that, gasping, ramming at me like a human firecracker.

'I didn't want to come too quickly so I made her get off, and then I grabbed her by the hips and bent her over the coffee table. She wiggled her bottom and I slid my prick between her bouncy buttocks and I was soon ramming her pussy from behind.

'Then she turned her head round and said: "I've got an even better idea," and I thought she simply wanted a regular face-to-face fuck. But instead she slid down on the carpet and splayed her legs wide. The quivering cheeks of her backside looked more inviting than ever and her love lips pouted even more tantalisingly. I lay down on top of her and gently pushed the tip of my cock inside her hot, wet cunt.

'It was very tight because Barbara was lying down and not on all fours, but once I'd managed to slide all of my throbbing tool inside her honeypot, it felt out of this world. She was squeezing my dick inside her by moving up and down and, as I thrust harder, the pressure grew and I could feel the warm mounds of her bum against my belly. My balls squashed against her and I slipped my arms round to play with her tits while my cock seemed to reach to the end of her cunt.

'"God, I love it, I love it!" she yelled and I couldn't hold back any longer and my cock twitched like crazy as I shot a jet of spunk deep inside her cunt. I lay on her for a few moments and then hauled myself up and looked at my watch. "I know this sounds very ungallant, but I have to be on my way," I said as she got up and gave me a couple of tissues from the box on the sideboard.

'"That's all right, Peter," she said as cool as a cucumber. "But if I give you my telephone number, I hope you'll come round and fuck me again one afternoon – I often work from home on Thursday afternoons so that's probably the best day to find me in. You will call, won't you? As you now know, I'm a passionate woman with many unsatisfied needs."

'It was wrong of me to ask such a personal question, but I couldn't help blurting out: "I'd love to, but what about your old man? I mean, he's not always away and to be frank with you, I don't like coming between husband and wife. I generally stay away from married women."

'Barbara chuckled and said: "Very noble of you, I'm sure, but you don't have any worries on that score, my dear. This may shock you but Alan knows all about my occasional gentleman friends and he doesn't mind at all. In fact, the only way he can get his cock up these days is for me to tell him about my randy adventures. So, far from wrecking our marriage, you'd be doing us both a great favour by coming round here and fucking the arse off me now and then."'

'I took her telephone number, but to be honest with you, I'm not sure whether I shouldn't call it a day and quit whilst I'm ahead, because despite what she says, you never know where you stand with married women. They're more fickle than single girls and there's always possible grief if there's still a husband sniffing around. For instance, if Barbara's old man starts performing between the sheets again, I might find myself the piggy in the middle and he could come after me with a baseball bat.

'Now you're a man of the world, Ivor. What's your opinion?'

Ivor considered the question with due seriousness before delivering a cautious judgement, as Peter accelerated over a yellow light at Hyde Park Corner and sped through down Constitution Hill towards Buckingham Palace.

'Yes, it would be sensible not to become too involved with Barbara,' Ivor advised as he noticed that the Royal Standard was flying over the Palace, which indicated that the Queen was in residence. I bet a few of the royals have been involved in some juicy leg-over situations, he thought to himself as he went on: 'But it wouldn't be fair if you didn't turn up for another two or three Thursday afternoon sessions. Let's face it, she treated you very handsomely, and it would be a bit unfeeling not to slip her a length a couple more times.

'But then if I were you, Pete, I'd say bye-bye to Barbara. You're quite right, long affairs with married women can cause trouble. Funnily enough, I'm involved in the launch of a new stay-hard cream for men called *Stallion*. One dab of this on your cock and you can fuck away like an eighteen-year-old. If Barbara's husband buys a tube and it does the trick for him, who knows what would happen as far as you're concerned?'

Peter swung left into The Mall and said: 'My point exactly – thanks, Ivor, I'm sure you're right. I'll screw her another couple of times and then disappear from the scene. Here, what's this new cream all about then? I might be interested in a tube. I don't mind telling you that after a hard day's driving in this lousy traffic, I'm not always feeling that fruity when I get home.'

'Give me your address and I'll send you a free sample of *Stallion*,' promised Ivor, and when they reached the junction of Theobald Street and John Street, just a hundred yards from Mandy Harcourt's office, Peter Ward refused to accept any payment from Ivor for taking him there. 'I was on my way home anyway,' he explained as he waved away Ivor's proferred pound note. 'And a tube of that stuff will be more than worth what's on the clock. See you around, Ivor, have a nice evening.'

Ivor looked at his watch and smiled – it was seven twenty-five exactly and he walked jauntily towards the new white building which housed the London head-quarters of Osbourne and Webb Associates. Mandy was already waiting for him in the foyer and she waved to him and then asked the night porter to open the door and let her out. As ever, Ivor thrilled at the sight of the long-legged, tousle-headed blonde girl and he quickened his stride to meet her and enveloped her in a firm bear-hug as their bodies melted together.

'Hello, love, hope you haven't been waiting long,' he said as they walked back arm in arm to the main road.

'No, you were nice and punctual, darling, and I'd only just left my desk,' she replied. 'How did your meeting go?'

'Okay, though between ourselves I think we may have a problem with one of Ruff's boyfriends,' said Ivor as he hailed a passing taxi, which skidded to a stop just a few yards ahead of them. After they had climbed into the taxi and Ivor had told the driver to take them to the Odeon, Leicester Square, Mandy asked him if there was anything specifically troublesome about the situation with Ruff.

Normally, Ivor would never mention anything about the singer's affairs to someone outside the inner circles of top management inside Cable Publicity and the Mackswell Organisation, but Mandy knew all about Ruff's secret life because her cousin was of the same sexual persuasion and had met the pop star at several private homosexual parties given by a prominent Conservative Member of Parliament in a private room at the House of Commons.

However, Ivor was careful not mention the blackmailing letter from Cliff Pendlebury and simply told Mandy how, against everyone's advice, Ruff had released a sub-standard single simply because his beloved had written the song which naturally had not sold as well as his previous records.

He went on: 'Now Cliff, his boyfriend, wants us to

spend more money hyping the song, but honestly, it would be chucking good money down the drain. I don't think I'll have problems explaining the situation to Ruff but I expect that Cliff will scream blue murder about how we're not doing enough for his precious song.'

'Yes, it could be difficult, but I'm afraid that you're not the only one with a problem to solve,' said Mandy as she opened her handbag and took out a sheet of paper. 'Ivor, do you remember those sexy photographs you took of me in your bedroom last month?'

Ivor grinned and said: 'You mean those shots I took with the camera Martin Reese gave me for signing up Ashberg Textiles? How could I ever forget that night, you silly sausage?'

'Well, I hate to tell you but someone at the office stole them from my handbag a few days ago,' she said miserably. 'I didn't know till yesterday because nothing else was taken, not even the ten pounds I had in my purse. But this morning I found this letter on my desk.'

She handed it to Ivor who read the typed missive:

Dear Mandy,

You are a very naughty girl to let your boyfriend take such rude pictures of you. But I'm glad he did because when I saw you in all your gorgeous nudity I nearly jerked my cock right off. You must be the hottest, horniest, most cock-hungry young lady that I've ever seen in my whole life. I'd like to take a whole week to fuck you senseless and I know you'd really enjoy that, especially in the photograph where

*you stick your bottom cheeks out towards the camera
with your legs apart so I can see both your cunt and
your little bum-hole. You look as if you're dying for
a thick prick to ram into your squelchy pussy from the
rear and fuck you with long, powerful strokes which
get louder and harder before depositing a hefty wad of
creamy cum inside your cunny. I'd love to go down on
you afterwards and lap up the lovely mix of spunk and
pussy juice from your cunt. Wouldn't that be nice?*

*When I'd finished I would rub honey all over your
beautiful breasts and lick every drop off your big,
strawberry tits before letting you tongue my throbbing
eight-and-three-quarter-inch cock which I would sink
into your sopping wet pussy and make love to you
real slow.*

*Then I'd get you on your hands and knees and ride
you from behind whilst playing with your firm breasts
and hard titties. Then I'd pull out and wank myself off
all over your backside whilst rubbing my knob over
your delicious bum cheeks.*

*M'mmm, just thinking about you is making my
cockshaft as hard as iron, especially as Beth Bristowe
has just walked past my door. This sets me wondering
whether the three of us could get together one of these
days. I would first sit back and watch you two play
with each other's titties until you would each come
over and suck my cock. Then I would take turns
fucking both of you doggy-style whilst the other was
on her knees sucking the other girl's pussy.*

*I know you've been going steady with that clever,
good-looking young chap Ivor Belling from Cable*

Publicity for the last few weeks, but perhaps next week I'll pluck up enough courage to ask one of you for a date. However, for now I'll just sign off as An Unknown Admirer.

'Well, what do you think?' demanded Mandy and Ivor gave her a lop-sided smile. 'He's a strange one, and no mistake. Whoever would want to measure his cock to the nearest quarter inch, and why would he want to finish himself off instead of coming inside you?'

'Oh, be serious, Ivor, I'm very upset. This letter's probably been typed on one of the IBM Golfball machines in the office, and we use this thick, plain paper for copies of important stuff, so I'm pretty sure someone at work is responsible.'

'Have you *any* idea who it could be?' enquired Ivor with an amused expression on his face. 'Whoever it is can't be all bad – look how he describes me!'

Mandy looked at him crossly and said: 'Ivor, you can be a real shit sometimes! Can't you see how upset I am about finding this letter on my desk after some very personal photographs were taken from my handbag!'

'Sorry, darling,' he apologised, trying to keep a straight face. 'But the situation isn't as bad as you think. For starters, look at the date at the top of the sheet.'

She tore the letter from him and read aloud: 'April the first . . . Oh, Ivor, it's an April Fool's Day joke! Well, that puts my mind at ease a little bit, but some toe-rag in my firm must have still sneaked into my bag and taken out the photographs, and I won't rest till I know who it was!'

'I've a pretty shrewd suspicion as to who the culprit is,' said Ivor soothingly. 'And no, I'm not guilty and if I'm right, it wasn't anybody in your office either.'

'Then who the hell stole those photographs?' she pouted and Ivor chuckled: 'Darling, you really are getting scatter-brained in your old age. No-one from Osbourne and Webb went to your handbag. Obviously, you've forgotten that you went down to Brian Lipman's studios to have a couple of the photographs of me enlarged to send to your sister in California and you must have left the whole set there.'

'Oh, of course, how stupid of me! I did leave them all with Brian. Hold on though, he wouldn't write to me like that, even as a joke!'

'No, of course he wouldn't,' said Ivor as he wrapped his arm around the angry girl and gave her a big cuddle. 'but I wouldn't put it past old Arthur, the guy who does all the developing at the studio. He's got a pretty weird sense of humour and I happen to know that he can type as he also does a lot of Brian's secretarial work. Come to think of it, there's an IBM Golfball typewriter in the studio. Someone used it for a set last year and Brian bought it for a song.

'Yup, Arthur's your man all right. The question now is do we confront him with the letter or tell Brian about it first?'

Mandy looked at him with a new respect in her eyes. 'Oh Ivor, you are so clever! That bloody letter has been bothering me ever since I clapped eyes on it. And incidentally, it arrived in the post and there was a Holborn post-mark on the envelope, so there's another piece of circumstantial proof against the old bastard!

'But what do you think we should do, darling? I don't fancy telling tales to Brian about what's happened.'

Ivor kissed her cheek. 'Why don't you leave it to me to have a quiet word with Brian? Actually, Arthur's supposed to retire in June and Brian won't be sorry if he can get him out before then. He would have given Arthur the push years ago but Mario, his partner, wouldn't hear of it because Arthur has worked for him since the end of the war.'

'Well, I don't want to cause trouble between Brian and Mario,' said Mandy doubtfully but Ivor reassured her. 'You'd be doing them both a favour. Christ, suppose Arthur had written that letter to a girl who worked for one of their biggest clients? The studio would be put out of business. As it happens, Arthur won't suffer as he'll be paid off, though he deserves to lose much more for being so idiotic. By the way, I'm bloody well going to see that he writes you an apology.

'Anyhow, at least we've solved the mystery,' he concluded as the taxi drew up outside the cinema. 'Now I'm sure that the film will give us both a good laugh and we'll forget all about this silly letter.'

The Wrong Box was a new, star-studded British film starring such luminaries as Ralph Richardson, John Mills, Wilfrid Lawson as well as newer stars like Michael Caine, Peter Cook and Dudley Moore. The reviews had been mixed but Ivor and Mandy thoroughly enjoyed the movie, a complicated black farce about two elderly Victorian brothers who try to murder each other in order to inherit a fortune.

'It shows you can't trust the critics,' said Mandy as they sat in the back of a cab heading towards her flat in West Kensington. 'I liked the film very much. Thanks again, Ivor, for taking me. It's as well you managed to get house seats, wasn't it, because the place was packed.'

'My pleasure,' said Ivor indistinctly as he buried his face between Mandy's breasts and she giggled: 'Sit up, darling, there'll be plenty of time after supper. Remember, Jilly's away so you can stay the night if you like. Mind, you don't have to if you don't want to!'

'I won't even grace that comment with a reply,' said Ivor and once inside Mandy's spacious, high-ceilinged apartment, he gathered her up in his arms and gave her a tremendous kiss.

She returned his kiss and they stood in the hall pressed closely together with their tongues threshing around in each other's mouths. Ivor slid his hands across her breasts which made Mandy wriggle in his arms. 'Oooh. don't do that, Ivor,' she begged as she rubbed her tummy sinuously against his bulging erection, 'Otherwise I'll never get supper started.'

'Blow supper,' muttered Ivor as he nibbled on her ear, but she pulled back from him and protested: 'I'm hungry, darling! *You* might have had a big business lunch but all I've had to eat since breakfast is an egg and cress sandwich and a Mars bar. Now I'll make us a nice mushroom omelette or, if you prefer, we could have some spaghetti with tomato sauce.'

Ivor kissed her ear and said: 'An omelette's fine, darling, but let me help you. Is there anything that I can do?'

'You can cut the tomatoes and cucumber for the salad,' answered Mandy, kissing him on the tip of his nose. 'And you can open the bottle of wine in the fridge and lay the table.'

'I can think of something nicer to lay,' he grunted and she let her hand fall to squeeze his cock as she murmured: 'So can I, but just remember we can fuck all night and I don't want to drain your balls too quickly.'

'No chance,' he smiled as he took off his jacket and loosened his tie. Despite his overwhelming ache to fuck Mandy, Ivor's cock gradually subsided into flaccidity whilst he watched her bustle around the kitchen as he prepared their salad. Unlike his previous girlfriend, Mandy was a good cook and Ivor relaxed and enjoyed the tasty, fluffy omelette and the freshly ground coffee with which they finished their meal.

However, when they had stacked the plates and cutlery in the dishwasher, he was more than ready when Mandy enquired if he were ready for bed. They went into the bedroom where Mandy began to undress whilst Ivor went into the bathroom. When he returned, Ivor stood still and he breathed heavily as he looked down at Mandy who was lying on her back on top of the bedclothes.

She had been blessed with a truly lovely body, from the soft tresses of golden blonde hair which fell down the sides of her pretty face to her small, perfectly formed feet. Her breasts were not large but her bosoms jutted out firmly and were topped by luscious, strawberry-red nipples which Ivor adored to suck. His eyes swivelled down across her flat, snow-white belly down to the glossy, flaxen mound of pussy hair and he passed his tongue over his lips as Mandy smoothed her hand between her thighs and let her fingers stray inside her silky pubic bush. She looked up directly at him as she playfully parted her love lips and began to frig herself gently, moving her fingertips slowly along the edges of her moistening slit.

Ivor tore off his clothes and threw himself down beside her on the bed and in a trice they were all over one another, squeezing and groping and giggling. He buried his face between her breasts, taking first one elongated nipple and then the other in his mouth as she cradled him to her.

'You are really the most delectable creature,' murmured Ivor as his lips travelled downwards and, resting his head on her thigh, he contemplated the voluptuous sexual delta in front of him. Mandy's pouting crack lay open and exposed beneath the golden thatch of pussy fur and his cock throbbed furiously against the inside of her leg as he gazed lasciviously at Mandy's fleshy cuntal lips which curled outward like butterfly wings, revealing the pink entrance to the tunnel within.

He applied his lips gently to Mandy's honeyed slot, blowing short, warm breaths through her silky blonde bush, making her squirm with pleasure. Then he started to lick her lightly from the base of her furrow up to the top of her slit, stopping just short of her clitty before travelling down again.

This sent Mandy wild with excitement and she thrust her pelvis down on Ivor's face, imprisoning his head in the fork of her thighs as he inhaled the musky perfume as she drenched his face in a spray of love juice.

'Oh yes, yes, yes!' she cried out as now Ivor found her hardened love button and rolled his tongue around this most sensitive area whilst he playfully nibbled at the rubbery, erectile flesh. Mandy writhed so frenziedly that Ivor found it impossible to keep his mouth on her twitching clitty and he pulled back his head and savoured the moment as he now mounted her, giving his pulsing prick a quick rub before guiding his knob between her yielding cunny lips, and Mandy raised her legs high in the air as he slid his cock inside her.

They made love with wild abandon and Ivor fucked the trembling girl in long, smooth strokes and his balls slapped in cadence against her backside as his cock squelched in and out of her clinging cunt. He groaned out loud as she sank her teeth into his shoulder and he pushed his fingertip inside her arsehole, and Mandy bucked madly back and forth as she revelled in the sensation of being double-fucked by his prick and finger filling her at the same time.

'I'm coming! I'm coming!' she yelled out happily as dizzying circles of pure ecstasy widened out from her pussy. 'Spunk into my cunny and fill me with your hot sticky cum!'

A shiver ran through Ivor's body as he plunged in his rampant shaft one final time, and his body began to shake as he spurted his seed inside her tingling cunt. This sent Mandy into fresh raptures of sheer bliss, launching her into a second shattering orgasm, and she shuddered all over whilst Ivor worked his cock in and out of her sodden love channel until the last drains of jism had been milked from his prick, which was now coated with Mandy's love juice.

He withdrew his deflated tadger and lay on his back with his arm around Mandy, who cuddled into the crook of his shoulder. 'M'mm, that so nice that I'd like some more, please. Now, I wonder whether I can make your soldier stand to attention?'

She slid her hand up and down Ivor's wet cock and delicately peeled the foreskin down to reveal his pink, gleaming helmet. To her great delight, his shaft began to swell in her grasp and very soon it stood up as thick and hard as before, and Mandy licked up a tiny pearl of juice which glistened in the tiny 'eye' on top of his knob.

'It's time to pay homage to the tower of power', she intoned as she continued to wank his throbbing cock, tracing her finger along the wide, blue vein whilst she squeezed and rubbed his hot, wet prick. Then Mandy lowered her head and in one swift movement she sucked his smooth, uncapped knob into her mouth. Her head bobbed up and down and then she ejected his prick from her lips with an audible plop.

'Oh, I say,' said Ivor disappointedly, but she placed a finger against his lips. 'Hush now, I promise that I'll suck you off later, but for now I want you to fuck me doggy-style.'

'Your wish is my command,' said Ivor in a grave tone

which made Mandy giggle as she slid over to lie on her tummy. He clambered up behind her as she hoisted herself onto her hands and knees and placed her head on one side on the pillow. With one hand, Ivor prised open a channel between the soft, round buttocks and with the other he held his now massively thick tool which pulsed with eagerness as it stood out rock-hard from its nest of curly brown hair.

Ivor slid his knob between Mandy's bum cheeks and slowly eased his knob and three or four inches of his shaft inside her juicy cunt.

'Is that too much cock for you?' he asked, but Mandy immediately gasped: 'No, darling, that's lovely, sink it in to the hilt. Oooh, that's marvellous, now just stay still for a few moments and let your cock stay there – please don't move a millimetre! Your knob is tickling my clitty beautifully!'

So Ivor stayed still for some fifteen seconds or so until he could not bear to wait any longer, and he began to fuck her with long, powerful strokes, cramming his pulsating prick inside her cunny as he leaned forward to fondle her breasts, his eyes bright with excitement as faster and faster he pistoned his shining, slippery shaft forwards and backwards out of her juicy honeypot.

Mandy now fell into his rhythm and started jerking her hips to and fro in time with Ivor's pumping so that with every thrust, her bottom smacked against his tummy and her pussy seemed to tighten its grip all the more, as if a suction pump had been applied to the helmet of Ivor's rampant prick. Suddenly the muscles of her cunny tightened about his shaft in a long,

163

rippling seizure which ran from the base of his prick to the very tip of his twiching tool. This clutching spasm sent his sperm roaring up from his balls and before Ivor could do more than utter a sharp groan, the spunk burst out of his cock and forced its way, warm and seething, into every nook and cranny of Mandy's cunt.

Gush after gush jetted out of his knob and Mandy's love channel quivered all round his shaft as she simultaneously climaxed with him. The muscular contractions of her pussy increased his pleasure to ecstatic proportions as his cock disgorged a final flow of hot, creamy jism, and then they fell forwards into an untidy heap as the enveloping pleasure of the fuck died slowly away.

Ivor reached down into her dripping wetness and rubbed the mix of their love juices over Mandy's succulent breasts. Nothing loath, she followed suit and plastered Ivor's chest with their cum as they lay entwined in an intimate muddle of arms and legs.

'Nice to come together, isn't it?' said Ivor as they gathered their strength after their exhausting erotic exercises.

'Oh yes, very nice indeed,' she agreed, nuzzling herself down against his taut, lean frame. 'Though in my opinion it isn't the be-all and end-all in good fucking. What matters most is having a partner who knows what he's doing and makes love with lots of tender, unselfish care.

'I'll tell you what I *don't* like, though, and that's a man asking me if I came or not. If I come, he should know well enough and if I don't, he can help bring me off later with his cock or his fingers.'

'And I'll tell you what I don't like,' said Ivor with as straight a face as he could muster, 'and that's girls who start sucking my cock and don't finish the job!'

Mandy squealed in mock horror. 'You cheeky sod! Wasn't it just as nice fucking me instead?'

A twinkle appeared in Ivor's eyes as he grinned and continued his teasing: 'Very much so, darling, but how shall I put it – if you go to a restaurant and order lamb chops, but the waiter brings you a lovely tender fillet steak instead, if your face was fixed for lamb chops, the steak won't taste quite as delicious.

'No, I'm not really complaining,' he added swiftly when he saw a frown appear on Mandy's forehead. 'I was only winding you up.'

'I'll wind you up, Ivor Belling, you and your cock,' she said as she grabbed hold of his flaccid shaft in her fist and started to slick her hand up and down, capping and uncapping his pink, round knob.

'I'll have a go, but I don't know whether I'm up to scoring three goals in an hour,' he said doubtfully and Mandy gave a throaty chuckle. 'Well, my love, there's only one way to find out. If Jimmy Greaves can net a hat-trick in twenty minutes . . .'

Ivor surrendered gracefully as Mandy laid him down on his back and bent forward over him, rubbing his rigid rod against her pert, uptilted breasts and squeezing its hot, blue-veined length between her luscious, soft bosoms. Then she moved across to straddle his body so that her peachy young backside was directly in front of his face as she lowered her head and parted her sweet lips to take Ivor's bursting cock into her deliciously wet mouth. She sucked slowly and deeply which brought a low, wrenching groan of ecstacy from him, and she bobbed her head backwards and forwards until she had slurped down almost all of his throbbing tool into her throat.

The cheeks of her bare bum wiggled provocatively in front of Ivor's eyes, and his groping fingers soon parted the moist lips of her juicy pussy and Mandy's buttocks jiggled lustfully as he forced his head upwards and slipped his tongue inside her wet crack, which made Mandy gasp as she continued to suck frantically on his pulsing prick. She wriggled her hips and the curled point of his tongue found her tiny wrinkled arsehole which made her shudder as her body exploded into a series of short, sharp climaxes, and her clitty squished against his fingers as they slipped in and out of her dripping cunt, coated with tangy love juice which trickled freely down her thighs.

Now she released his twitching tadger from her mouth and slid nimbly across his body to lie on her back next to him with her long legs parted and her fingers inside her pussy, spreading apart the pouting, pinky lips of her juicy honeypot.

He scambled up on his knees to place himself between her legs. Resting on his elbows he looked down upon Mandy's thrilling curves which glistened with perspiration. Her eyes were closed and she was breathing heavily as she reached out blindly for his prick, which she grasped with both hands and guided into her lush cunny.

Mandy raised her legs high in the air as he came

into her, and at once they were locked into a hard, sweeping rhythm as Ivor fucked her in long, smooth strokes, and his balls slapped in cadence against her bottom as he moved up and down, rubbing her stalky nipples as his cock squelched in and out of her sopping love channel. He let himself be enveloped in her frenzy, glorying in the smooth motion of her hips which moved at an ever increasing speed, and Ivor felt his cock swell even further inside Mandy's cunt as she kept driving up against the power of his thrusts, bouncing up to meet him over and over again as she eagerly met every fresh onslaught, crossing her legs to trap his shaft inside her tingling cunny.

'I'm coming! I'm coming! Oh, yes, I'm there, darling!' she yelled out happily, and she bucked wildly as Ivor ejaculated whilst he plunged his prick deep inside her tingling cunt, and she arched her back to receive the thick squirts of spunk which spurted out of his cock into her love funnel.

'Phew, what an exhausting fuck,' said Mandy brightly as she wiped the perspiration from her forehead. 'Do give my kindest regards to your cock and tell him that I hope he enjoyed that fuck as much as I did.'

Ivor lifted up his head and kissed her nipples. 'I'll pass on your kind message as soon as I get my breath back,' he sighed as he closed his eyes.

They stayed still for a few minutes and then Mandy clicked her fingers and said: 'Ivor, wake up, darling! There's something I want to show you.'

'It can't be as interesting as what I've already seen tonight,' said Ivor sleepily, but Mandy rolled over and picked up an envelope from the beside table. 'I'm serious, Ivor, please sit up and read this letter which came through the letter-box a couple of days ago.'

From the tone of her voice, he could tell that Mandy wasn't joking so he heaved himself up and took hold of the sheet of paper. 'What's all this about? You've already shown me one letter this evening – '

'Yes, I know, darling, but this letter wasn't for me. It was addressed to Jilly Barnes, my new flat-mate. You met her for a minute last Sunday when you picked me up to go to lunch with your married friends, Abigail and Jonathan. She's a tall, very attractive girl with a gorgeous figure who works for a wholesale fashion house in Great Titchfield Street.'

'Oh sure, she's quite a looker, isn't she? Now don't tell me she's also getting anonymous sexy letters.'

Mandy shrugged her shoulders. 'Not quite, but you're pretty close. If the letter were anonymous, I don't think it would trouble Jilly that much, but the trouble is that it came from her boss.'

'Her boss?' he echoed in surprise. 'That's very strange. Surely the guy could get himself into a heap of trouble. Why, he'd probably get the sack himself if Jilly reported him to someone higher up the ladder.'

She shook her head and said: 'I'm afraid that wouldn't work, darling. You see, Jilly's boss owns the whole flaming company!'

'Oh, that does make it a bit awkward, then. Well, I'd better see what the silly bugger has got to say for himself,' said Ivor as he scanned the hand-written letter, and he noted that Jilly's employer had made no attempt to hide his identity for on the headed notepaper underneath *Albion Fashions* was printed a line: *From The Desk of Philip Hughes, Managing Director*. Ivor now slowly read the letter which began:

Dearest Jilly,

As you know, I don't beat about the bush, so I'll come straight to the point. When you come into work tomorrow, in the bottom drawer of your desk you will find a small parcel. What I want you to do is to take the parcel into the ladies cloakroom and change into the chambermaid's costume you will find inside it. The reason for this request is simple: you remind me very much of Helga, a young chalet maid I had the pleasure of meeting last year whilst on a ski-ing holiday in Switzerland. She had the same firm, high breasts and glossy dark hair as you and the same smouldering sex appeal which, out of all the girls who work for me, only you possess.

Helga was a cheeky young girl, perhaps two or three years younger than you, who I first met whilst she was bending over to pick up the waste-paper basket in my bedroom and, as her black skirt was very short, I was given a wonderful view of her frilly white knickers which were stretched tight over her bum cheeks. My prick stiffened up immediately at this luscious sight but I was sure that although Helga must have known full well that I had come into the room, she had deliberately waited for a few seconds before straightening up.

My suspicions were confirmed the next afternoon when I came back to the chalet after a hard day's ski-ing. I stripped off and went into the bathroom for a shower. Whilst I was drying myself I thought I heard a noise inside the bedroom, which was strange as I had shut the door behind me. So I stepped out of the bathroom wearing nothing but a towel around my shoulders to investigate. And there in the middle of the room, was Helga wearing her short black dress with a white apron, holding a feather duster in her hand, and this gave me an instant hard-on.

I thought this might scare her but Helga never took her eyes of my naked body and I could clearly see her nipples straining against her dress. She stretched out her hand and pulled away my towel and she proceeded to give me a brisk rub-down till I was tingling all over and then, still without speaking but with a saucy twinkle in her eye, she dropped the towel on the floor and picked up the feather duster.

'Ach so,' she murmured as she ran the duster all over my chest and then teasingly down lower until it was brushing my throbbing chopper. She tickled all round my knob until the jism came shooting out.

This experience was certainly the highlight of my holiday and I'd love to see you brandish a feather duster in the way that Helga did! Naturally, I would be pleased to make it worth your while.
Yours hopefully,
Philip

Ivor put down the letter and handed it back to Mandy. 'Who is this crazy guy?' he demanded hotly. 'The man's a raving idiot. If dynamite were brains, he wouldn't have enough to blow the wax out of his ears! Does he really believe that a nice girl like Jilly would take any notice of a letter like that?

'I mean to say, if he gets his rocks off with feather dusters, all well and good. But doesn't he realise how insulting it is to Jilly to simply barge in and make what's basically a business proposition to her? Where's his imagination, his sense of style, his – '

Mandy tugged his ear-lobe and interrupted him. 'Yes, Ivor, of course you're quite right, darling, but the point is what should poor Jilly do about it?'

'Simple, give in her notice and look for another job straight away,' said Ivor without any hesitation. 'And if this chap won't give her a great reference, she should simply tell him that she'll photocopy the letter and send it all round the rag trade – assuming of course that she's been offended by the letter. Is this Mr Hughes a nice man to work for?'

'Not really,' said Mandy as she put the letter back in the envelope. 'He has one of these new MBA business degrees and Jilly says it must stand for management by antagonism because he's so nasty to people, throwing his weight around, you know the type.'

Ivor scratched his head and asked: 'So why didn't she leave even before she received this silly letter?'

'Well, Jilly's not just a secretary, you know. She earns good money because she's also a showroom model, and jobs aren't that easy to get, even though she's a perfect size ten. Jilly's not well off and she needs a well-paid job. She's a damned good typist and can take short-hand.'

'Then I don't see any problem – Jilly should simply

ignore the man till she finds herself something better or, if she doesn't want to face him again, she can fix herself up with temporary work whilst she looks around. Mind, I'm sure the guy's quite harmless, or he wouldn't sign the letter, would he?'

'I suppose so,' she admitted as she put the letter back on the bedside table. 'Jilly's a bright girl, Ivor. Would you have any jobs going for her in your office?'

'There's nothing at present as far as I know but I'll check with Julia, our office manager, and if there's anything of interest, she'll give Jilly a call to come up for an interview.'

'Thanks, Ivor, you're a pal. I'll tell Jilly as soon as she gets back,' said Mandy, kissing him on the cheek. 'Now, let's see if your cock is ready to salute me again, or are you going to look a gift horse in the mouth?'

God, I'd give a tenner for a tube of *Stallion* thought Ivor as, with a glassy smile, he settled himself down as Mandy's head dived between his legs and she began to lick his balls.

Whilst Ivor was summoning his reserves of stamina, Martin Reese was enjoying a quiet, after-dinner drink with Katie Sheldon, the editor of the *Daily Globe* women's page, at the Hunkiedorie Club, and the managing director of Cable Publicity was taking the opportunity to plug *Stallion* erection cream to her.

'Sounds to me as if you could be on to a winner there, Martin,' said Katie Sheldon with interest. 'Listen, as soon as *Stallion* is in the shops, let me know and I promise I'll run a big piece about this new wonder drug which can revolutionise your bedroom life.'

'Thanks very much, Katie,' said Martin, waving his hand at a waiter and ordering two more large cognacs. 'But there are no drugs in *Stallion*, it's made out of purely herbal ingredients, though I dare say it wouldn't do you any good to swallow the stuff.'

His guest chuckled hoarsely and said: 'That reminds me of a good story I heard in New York last month, Martin. An Irishman goes to the doctor and says: "Can you help me, sor, I have the most terrible constipation." The doctor pulls open a drawer and takes out a packet of suppositories and says: "Here you are, Paddy, these will get you going." Well, a week later, the Irishman returns to the surgery and the doctor says: "Well, everything back to normal?" but Paddy shakes his head and says: "No, sor, I'm afraid not, I'm still in trouble – and as for those pills you gave me, for all the good they've done I might as well have stuck them up my arse!"'

Martin laughed heartily as the waiter placed their drinks on the table. As he left them Katie leaned forward and said: 'Old Bernie's a useful contact, you know, he's given me two or three good tip-offs about the goings-on of some of the minor royals, but he's not a patch on the smashing young waiter I met in New York!'

'You had a good time in New York, Katie? Was it your first time there?' asked Martin.

'No, I went over two years ago and I've enjoyed myself immensely both times. Manhattan's such a vibrant city. It's alive and pulsing twenty-four hours a day, every day,' she replied as she picked up her glass and sipped the smooth, fiery liqueur. 'Mind you, I had to work bloody hard on this last trip, interviewing showbiz stars and checking out some material for the fashion pages. Well, one afternoon I had a long interview with Phil Silvers, you know, the man who played Sergeant Bilko in the TV series. He's coming to Britain next year, by the way, to star in a *Carry On* film.

'Anyway, he was pretty hard going and I was quite tired by the time we finished, so I decided to treat myself and have dinner at the Trattoria Calabro, a smart Italian restaurant on West 48th Street which a friend had recommended to me.

'Even though it was only seven-thirty when I arrived there, the restaurant was quite crowded, but I was told I would only have to wait ten minutes for a table so I sat at the bar and ordered myself a campari and soda. And then, just as I was looking around admiring the intimate decor, with every table covered by a red-and-white checkered cloth on which stood candles and flowers, and thinking what a shame that here I was all alone in such a charming place, who should tap me on the shoulder but Sid Cohen!'

A wide grin settled over Martin's face and he said: 'Sid Cohen of Gee Girl Fashions? What a coincidence! I suppose he was in New York to look at the new season's styles. I've known Sid for years. He's a nice guy even though I haven't managed to win the PR account for the chain of Gee Girl boutiques he's setting up.'

'Well, now would be a very good time to pitch for the business, Martin,' Katie advised him. 'Sid's not exactly enamoured with his publicity people. He told me that all his competitors seem to get more column inches in the press than his business does.'

'Bless you, Katie, I'll contact Sid first thing tomorrow morning,' said Martin gratefully. Tell me, though, did he join you for dinner?'

'Yup, and then, as we were having coffee, he invited me to go with him to Julian's, a new, very exclusive disco on Fifth Avenue. "You are a broadminded girl, aren't you?" he asked and when I pinched his cheek and said I was game for almost anything, he added: "Okay, Katie, let's go. I want to see the cabaret at Julian's, it's supposed to be the hottest show in town."

'So after Sid won the fight about who should pay the bill (I must confess that I didn't put up too much resistance!) we strolled down the three blocks to Fifth Avenue. There was quite a crowd milling around outside the front door of Julian's, but the two large doormen in glittering gold coats were refusing entrance to all but a select few.

'"How do you know we will be able to get in?" I asked anxiously as Sid guided me through the crowd, but he told me not to worry as he fished out a card from his wallet and said that he had been given a personal invitation for himself and a guest by one of the club's directors, and that we would have no problem. And this proved to be the case as one of the doormen took the card from Sid and swung open the door for us. Inside the club, we were bowled over by the pounding beat of the music and flashing psychedelic lights. Sid had told me that a lot of models and showbiz people came to Julian's and certainly the circular dance floor was packed with gorgeous girls and good-looking young men. We were shown to a small table and Sid ordered a bottle of wine.

'"Well, now we're here, let's dance," I said as the disc jockey changed the mood and played a slow, bluesy number and, whilst we were on the floor, Sid suddenly whispered to me: "Look over to you right, Katie, isn't that Johnny Crawford of The Wards of Court giving one of his fans what she wants?"

'I peered over and sure enough there was the great Scottish rock singer dancing with a nubile young teen-ager whose arms were around his neck and who was pressing herself against him so that she could feel his groin rubbing against her tummy. They were quite oblivious to the noise and the people all around them, and Johny began to caress her breasts as they kissed open-mouthed whilst swaying together to a rhythm of their own.

'"Are you sure those two aren't the cabaret?" I said to Sid who shook his head and said: "Not if the stories I've heard are to be believed. Anyhow, the show doesn't start till well after midnight."

'By about one o'clock the place was still crowded when suddenly the music stopped and the disc jockey asked everyone to return to their seats as it was now cabaret time. "Please welcome Merida and Leroy!" he called out as the lights dimmed and then a spotlight picked out a sultry blonde girl in the centre of the dance floor who was wearing a black leather miniskirt topped off with a plunging white blouse which was pulled tightly over her breasts. Moments later she was joined by a lithe black man dressed only in a pair of hip-hugging running shorts. He was a handsome chap, coffee-coloured with a broad, manly chest and a slim youthful waist.

'The music started up again and the pair gave one of the most sensuous performances of modern dancing I have ever seen, it was so primal the way their bodies writhed and undulated that I began to feel sexy myself and I squeezed Sid's thigh under the table! Then, to the accompaniment of *The House of the Rising Sun* by The Animals, Merida unbuttoned her blouse and shrugged it off over her shoulders. Her firm, bare breasts jiggled as next she unzipped her skirt and wriggled it down to her ankles and she stepped out of it completely naked, revealing a beautifully flat belly and a fluffy little blonde bush which lightly covered her pouting pink cunny lips.

'Then, as Leroy stood stock still to a round of applause, Merida tugged down his shorts and I'm sure I wasn't the only woman there who gasped at the size of his amazingly long, thick prick which was just slightly erect enough to show off his big balls which swung as he pirouetted around Merida who stood still in a classical pose whilst Leroy knelt in front of her, his muscular arms like dark marble, kissing her lovely pussy. His shaft started to swell upwards until it was almost flat up against his belly, and then she hoisted him up by his shoulders so that they were locked together in a tight embrace with only his powerful prick between them, and Merida slid her hands down to grasp his enormous tool, sliding her fist up and down his veiny chopper.

'Meanwhile he ran his fingers through her pussy hair and she opened her legs wide to enable him to insert three fingers between her cunny lips, and in a flash they were both down on the floor in a *soixante neuf*, with Leroy on his back and Merida with her bum just over his face and, as she leaned forward to begin licking his knob, he parted her bum cheeks and began lapping at her pussy.

'"My God! She sure knows how to suck a cock!" said Sid quietly as we watched Merida open her lips and engulf his monster shaft. She bobbed her head up and down as she cupped his heavy balls, massaging them gently, lifting and separating each one as she slid her lips up and down his glistening prick.

'Just as the record finished Leroy came in her mouth and she swallowed all his jism to a great round of applause. Then they dashed off the stage and two new girls came on and did some very naughty things with a double-headed dildo, but I'd better not tell you any more, Martin, because you'll get over-excited! I know I did! In fact, after they'd finished, I said to Sid that I didn't want to stay for the next act but would prefer to go back to his hotel suite. But between ourselves, Sid was too tired to perform and even though I tried giving him a gobble, he couldn't get it up, poor love. He was okay in the morning, though, but we only had time for a quick knee-trembler before breakfast.'

'I'll casually mention *Stallion* to Sid,' said Martin thoughtfully and he offered Katie another drink, but she shook her head and said: 'No, I really must get going. Truth to tell, I'm feeling horny as hell now and a sweet little messenger boy from *The Globe* newsroom will be coming up to my flat after he's finished the evening shift. Many thanks for the drinks, Martin. Will I see you at the party down in Brighton for the launch of Ronnie Bloom's autumn collection?'

'Yup, I'll be there and I'm delighted that you're going, Katie, Ronnie's come up with some great ideas,' said Martin, who never missed an opportunity to promote his clients' products. 'Mark my words, he's got a new range of maxi-skirts which are going to hit the headlines.'

Katie kissed Martin on the cheek and left him nursing the last drains of his cognac. 'Bye love,' he said absently as the waiter ambled over and picked up Katie's empty glass.

'Nice woman, Miss Sheldon. Good-looking girl, too. I wouldn't mind having her warm my bed,' said the waiter and Martin grunted: 'Neither would I, Bernie, especially tonight when my wife's away in Wolverhampton on some wretched conference or other and it looks like I'll have wasted the opportunity for some on-the-side rumpy pumpy.'

Bernie gave him a large wink. 'Not necessarily, Mr Reese, Andrea's having a drink with Mr Decopoulos in the club tonight and you must know how much she fancies you. Why don't you join them in the bar?'

For a moment, Martin was tempted by the thought of cuddling up next to the luscious body of Andrea

Takalandrou, but then he quickly decided against following up Bernie's idea. For Andrea was the youngest sister of the owner of the Hunkiedorie Club, a large Greek Cypriot named Nedis Decopoulos, who was the head of a large family clan, most of whom were employed by him.

Andrea's ex-husband had worked as a barman at the Club until one day he had been caught cheating with one of the hostesses. Since then he had never been seen again and a rumour soon spread round the employees of the Hunkiedorie that the last time anyone had seen the poor man was when his body had been tipped into a cement mixer on a big construction site in Fulham.

'I think I'll pass, thank you,' Martin muttered quietly to Bernie. 'I wouldn't want to cause any family upsets, especially where the Decopoulos's are concerned.'

As he finished, Martin jumped as a large hand fell on his shoulder and his heart leaped when he spun round to see that it was none other than Nedis Decopoulos himself who had walked up behind him.

'Hello, Martin, how are you keeping? Now am I mistaken or did I hear my name being taken in vain?' he said in a friendly tone of voice.

Immediately Martin decided to tell the truth rather than be caught out later in a prevarication. 'No, you're not mistaken, Nedis,' he answered as he sank back into his chair. 'It's just that Bernie suggested I should go to the bar and chat to Andrea, but though she's a very nice girl and I like her a lot, I said I'd stay here as I wouldn't want anyone from your family to get any wrong ideas.'

'Very thoughtful of you, Martin, and I appreciate it,' said the club owner, snapping his fingers for Bernie. 'You must have a drink with me, I insist,' and he ordered two more cognacs.

'To be frank with you, I would have been only too pleased if you had come along to the bar,' he continued as he drew his chair closer to Martin's and he leaned forward as he quietly went on: 'Look, we're both men of the world and you know as well as I do that Andrea doesn't want to live in a nunnery for the rest of her life. She's very keen on a young man named Takis from Nicosia, but it's taking the devil of a time to arrange for a work permit so that he can stay in England. In fact, he's had to enrol as a student, and he won't be able to come over to London till the autumn. Meanwhile, Andrea needs a decent man to share her bed now and then, and a gentleman like yourself would be perfect for her because you could satisfy all her needs.'

Martin was flattered but slightly puzzled by this glowing testimonial and he asked: 'Why someone like me, though?'

Nedis Decopoulos smiled and said: 'Now you surprise me, Martin, isn't it obvious? You'll be good to her, you won't try to steal her money and, above all, you'll be discreet. There's an old Greek saying: a married man will never reveal an indiscretion but a single boy will talk about you.

'So, I would be extremely pleased if you would go into the bar and talk to my young sister. Hopefully, you will take her home and make mad, passionate love to her all night, because I know she needs a man to look after her needs until Takis arrives here in September. Then, of course, I will expect you to disappear from the scene and if I decide that the young man is good enough for my sister, they will get married and I will buy them a house in Wood Green. If not, I will send him back to Cyprus and look for somebody else.

'Now I have fully explained the situation to you, I hope that you will reconsider your decision. Ah, but you don't even have to move out of your chair, here comes Andrea now. She must have wondered where I had gone to.'

Martin looked across the room and saw Nedis's sultry, voluptuous sister had left the bar and was making her way across to them. He rose to his feet and smiled weakly as Andrea walked towards him. She was a stunningly attractive girl with long, shiny black hair which was cut with a fashionable fringe and swung glossily down her back. She was wearing a short, tight-fitting powder-blue dress which accentuated her full breasts and long tanned legs and Martin gulped as he kissed her proffered hand.

'Ah, a true gentleman,' she exclaimed lightly. 'Martin, I haven't seen you for ages – what have you been doing with yourself?'

Before he could answer her, Nedis stood up and said: 'Will you two please excuse me, I have some business to attend to in the restaurant.'

Andrea smiled as Nedis hurried away and said: 'My brother is not the most subtle of men, Martin, please don't feel obliged to stay with me.'

'Oh, but I'd love to, Andrea,' he replied truthfully,

now secure in the knowledge that far from being angry, Nedis Decopoulos would actually be grateful if he took Andrea to bed. 'What would you like to drink?'

'A black coffee would be fine, thank you,' she said as Bernie sidled up, and Martin decided to join her for even a liberal application of *Stallion* would have no effect if he ordered a third cognac, for both Martin and Ivor (unlike Craig Grey) suffered from brewers' droop and could only drink sparingly if they wanted to perform between the sheets at the peak of their sexual prowess.

And it was only minutes after Bernie had brought them their coffees that the subject of their conversation turned to sex. 'I'm not ashamed to say that I have needs,' said Andrea warmly. 'This is 1966 and the times are long gone when girls were supposed to lie back on their marriage beds and think of England whilst their husbands had their wicked ways with them.

'Mind you, I was educated at St Trippett's, a very old-established posh girls' boarding school in Warwickshire, and sex education didn't consist of very much more than very similar advice! Not that it stopped most of us losing our cherries by the time we had left the school. I remember one Founders Day when a group of us from the Lower Sixth pulled the gardener's boy and his friend into the changing rooms on the far side of the hockey pitches. My God, those poor lads must have had very sore cocks by the time we had finished with them!'

'At least you didn't miss out completely by being educated at an all-girls school,' commented Martin with a wry expression on his face. 'I was also sent to boarding school and there the only sexual activity we could indulge in was with Mother Thumb and her Four Daughters.'

Andrea giggled and said: 'Yes, surprisingly, it's often more difficult for boys to cross the Rubicon than girls. Not that there's anything wrong with masturbation. The other evening I was reading a book by Madge Tannenbaum, one of these American radical feminists who believes that intercourse itself is degrading because a man's thrusting of his prick into a woman's pussy is taken to be her capitulation to him as a conqueror.'

Martin frowned and said: 'What utter nonsense! I'm all for sexual equality but this woman must be a raving lesbian who simply hates men! For a start, how would we have managed to procreate over thousands and thousands of years if fucking were degrading? Women would have simply refused to mate – and these days, especially, girls are less frightened to tell their lovers what turns them on and they take charge of the fuck. For instance, quite a few girls I know enjoy taking a dominant position during sex by sitting on their men and bouncing up and down on their cocks.'

The sultry girl nodded her head in agreement and said: 'That's true, Martin, but from your own experience you won't deny that masturbation can be, now how did Madge Tannenbaum describe it, oh yes, one of the greatest sources of sexual pleasure, a release from tension and a delicious sedative before sleep.'

'I know an even sweeter sedative before sleep which I would be delighted to demonstrate to you,' said Martin thickly and to his delight Andrea responded by reaching across and squeezing his thigh.

'What a splendid idea, darling. Your place or mine?' she said briskly and as Andrea lived only a few minutes away in Mayfair, Martin eagerly agreed to go back to her splendid apartment in a luxurious block of flats just off Park Lane.

Once inside Andrea's apartment, Martin helped her take off her coat and he tossed it on to a chair. Coming up behind her he pushed her silky dark tresses aside and nuzzled his lips against the nape of her neck as he slowly unzipped the back of her dress. It slipped down to her waist and Martin eased it over her hips so that it fell to her feet. Next he unhooked her bra and Andrea herself slid the straps off her shoulders and threw it down on to the lush green carpet.

Martin looked at the luscious girl who was now wearing only a pair of frilly white panties and, with a throaty growl, he spun her round and pulled her to him and, as they kissed open-mouthed, his hands cupped her bare breasts as if weighing them. He teased her big brown nipples until they became hard and vibrant, all the time grinding his hips against her so that she could feel his throbbing erection pressed against her.

Andrea took hold of Martin's hand and led him into the bedroom where she kissed him again whilst she helped him tear off his clothes. When he was completely naked, she tugged down her knickers and whispered to him: 'Would you like to see me play with myself?'

Without waiting for an answer, she lay on the bed and slowly opened her legs, stroking the insides of her thighs with her hands. Then she drew one index finger through her black pubic curls as she kept her eyes fixed firmly on Martin's pulsing prick. Her finger now probed more deeply inside the red chink, making slow, circular movements around her clitty, gradually increasing the speed as she inserted two more fingers inside her slippery crack and began rubbing herself off in hard, rhythmic strokes.

This erotic sight sent Martin wild with desire and when Andrea beckoned him to join her, he threw himself on top of the gorgeous girl and immediately she took hold of his thick, circumcised shaft and guided it between her pouting pussy lips.

'A-a-h-r-e! A-a-h-r-e! A-a-h-r-e!' Andrea gasped as she bucked and squirmed under the fierce, surging strokes of Martin's sinewy cock, and she arched her back upwards to allow him to slide his hands under her fleshy, soft bum cheeks as he worked his hips in ever quickening rhythm whilst his prick squelched forwards and backwards inside her juicy love channel.

She whimpered with delight as she felt his cock swell even further inside her tingling sheath as she drove her body upwards to meet the power of his pistoning thrusts, bouncing back from each encounter and meeting each onslaught with a little yelp of delight.

Their climax was coming and Andrea whispered that he should come inside her. She felt the wonderful floating feeling of an approaching orgasm as Martin's thick prick touched the deepest places in her cunt.

'Oh yes, yes, YES!' she repeated over and over in a low, driving tone as he pushed inside her, and now his fingers were rolling and pinching her nipples in the same quickening rhythm of his thrusting. Then her taut, polished body exploded as Martin's cock spurted out a fountain of sticky white jism and she shuddered violently as the force of her own climax rocketed through her body while Martin continued to discharge the contents of his balls inside her.

When he finally withdrew his deflated shaft, Andrea leaned forward to plant a wet kiss on his shining knob. 'Oooh, that was marvellous, Martin,' she cooed as she lay back again with her hand between her legs, gently rubbing along the length of her crack. 'Now, I overheard two of the girls at the Hunkiedorie talking about how good you are at muff-diving. Will you send me to heaven again by eating my pussy?'

'Of course I will,' he replied gallantly and without hesitation he tucked his head between her thighs and kissed her sopping slit. Martin noted how Andrea had neatly trimmed her silky thatch which made the pouting pink pussy lips more prominent and more accessible to his tongue.

Andrea shuddered as he licked the outside of each lip in turn, a groan of pleasure rising from her throat and bursting like a bubble in the silence when he inserted his thumb inside her cunt and ran it along the full length of her cleft. Her body jerked at his touch and the soft walls of her gaping pussy sucked in his finger, whilst the tiny nub of her clitty stood proudly visible as Martin's tongue now sought out the secrets of her cunny.

Martin let his tongue work all over her erect, fleshy clitty and, as he nipped at it playfully with his teeth, she started to writhe and moments later her whole body convulsed and the waves of orgasm coursed through her, hot love juice filling Martin's mouth as he struggled to hold her steady during the repeated electric surges of her passion.

He sucked harder and harder, rolling his tongue round and round, lapping the tangy juices which were now spurting out from Andrea's cunt and, with a final scream, she came in great juddering spasms, splattering Martin's face and filling his mouth with her love juice which he swallowed whilst Andrea shuddered into limpness as her delicious crisis melted away.

Now Martin sat astride her and placed his rigid rod between her spread breasts. Andrea guessed what he wanted and she clutched at his satin-smooth shaft, pushing it between her ample bosoms and pressing her boobs over his cock, hiding it deep in her warm flesh as his shaft slid smoothly to and fro in the creamy ravine between her sumptuous breasts with his swollen purple knob appearing rhythmically beneath her chin.

'Ohhh! Ohhh! Ohhh!' moaned Martin as he pumped his cock backwards and forwards. 'That's *fantastic*, darling!'

Andrea's head rolled from side to side with her eyes half-closed, and then she stuck out her tongue to bestow long licks on the top of his knob with each up-thrust. Then she opened her mouth and muttered: 'Go on, you randy fucker, hurry up and cream my tits!'

He obeyed almost at once, squirting his sticky spunk into a pale, shining pool which she rubbed into her breasts with a blissful smile upon her face.

Martin rolled off her and Andrea gave his shrunken prick a friendly cuddle in her fist as she said: 'Oh, Martin, you do know how to make a girl happy. Thank you so much for fucking me. It's been so long since I had a thick, fat prick up my cunt that I thought I might have forgotten how to screw, but I started to come like a tornado as soon as you slid your cock between my cunny lips.'

'Hey, I'm not taking all the credit, you're pretty damned good yourself,' protested Martin. 'It takes two to tango, you know.'

He looked at her curiously and said: 'Andrea, forgive my asking a personal question, but haven't you made love with anyone since Takis left?'

She cocked her head as she considered her answer. 'Not with another man, Martin – you're the first since Takis – but I did have a rather interesting experience with a model girl called Delia earlier this year.'

Martin placed his elbow on the bed and rested his head in his hand. 'Hey, don't tell me you mean Delia Chumleigh from the Churchmill Agency? Ivor Belling's used her quite a few times when we've needed a pretty girl for some promotional work.'

'I know that,' said Andrea, leaning down to kiss his right nipple. 'In fact that's how I met Delia, because Nedis asked Cable to prepare a publicity pamphlet for the club and Ivor chose her to be featured in the leaflet as a Hunkiedorie hostess.'

'Oh yes, I remember now. Didn't Brian Lipman set up the shoot early one morning at the club?'

'That's right, and Nedis asked me to be there and

supervise the session for him. Well, Brian decided to dress Delia in a tight white mini-dress and believe me, Martin, she looked terrifically sexy in it. She's only nineteen with light green eyes, smooth pale skin and sulky pouting lips and I could see that Brian fancied her like crazy.

'"Are you and Delia going to have a scene together?" I asked him and he rolled his eyes upward and groaned. "Chance would be a fine thing," he said bitterly. "But Delia's a lezzie and won't let any man near her. Terrible waste of talent if you ask me, but what can you do?"

'The shoot went well but just as Brian was taking the last shots, the telephone rang and it was his studio on the line with an important message for him. It seems that Brian had left some contact sheets in his case and the client desperately needed to see them in the next hour.

'"Girls, I'm a right idiot – will you forgive me? I must dash round to Knightsbridge and show these prints to a fellow before he leaves for Paris this afternoon," he said. "I'll come back for my equipment when I get back – I shouldn't be much more than an hour or so. Andrea, I know you're a keen photographer. Everything's set up. There are seven more shots on this film, so if you'd like to try your hand at my job, be my guest!"

'I was quite taken with the idea, especially when Delia said that she had no objections. Anyhow, Brian rushed away and left us to it and he hadn't been gone five minutes before Delia said to me: "You know, I'm sure that Brian has plenty of good shots of me in this dress. What I really need are some good glamour shots for my portfolio. Would you take them for me, Andrea? I'd much rather be photographed in the nude by a girl than a guy."

"'Of course I will," I said and quick as a flash she stripped off until she was wearing nothing but a miniscule pink G-string around her waist with a miniature heart-shaped pouch which covered her pussy and two minute straps that slid into the crevice between her bum cheeks.

'She looked so sexy that I felt my nipples harden against my shirt as she posed provocatively on a *chaise longue*. "Open your legs a bit further, Delia," I instructed her as I squinted into the viewfinder of Brian's Rolleiflex. "Now rub your nipples. Get them really hard so they stick out."

'I clicked away and finished the film, and then I looked up and asked Delia if she would like a coffee as I'd made a pot before we began and left it to simmer when we began our work.

"'Thank you, that would be lovely," she said and to my surprise she made no attempt to get dressed but simply sat down next to me on the sofa, stark naked except for her tiny G-string. We chatted for a bit and then she put down the coffee cup and said in a suggestive voice: "Did Brian tell you that I prefer girls to guys?"

'I nodded and said: "Sure he did, but so what? Each to their own, that's always been my motto."

"'I'm glad to hear you say that, Andrea, because ever since you came in I've been terribly attracted to you. In fact, I'm already so wet that your hand would slip right up my cunt without any problem." And as she said this she put her hand on my thigh and I began to feel a definite wetness inside my panties.

'She was certainly forward for such a young girl because she reached over and took hold of my coffee cup which was trembling in my hands and placed it on the table. Then she leaned forward and started to kiss me hard, thrusting her tongue inside my mouth in a lip-smacking embrace.

'Then Delia shifted in her seat so that she was leaning over me, pushing her tits next to mine so that our nipples were touching. I could feel her hand moving to my damp pussy, and automatically I lifted my bum so that she could pull down my panties before brushing her fingers through my bush.

'"Oooooh!" I gasped as her index finger found my clitty and I leaned back on the sofa as she flicked the hard bud around.

'"You've made my hand all wet," Delia giggled as the first dribbles of juice ran over her fingers, and I thrust my hips and pussy up further so that she could get three fingers in and fill me up properly. She diddled my clitty beautifully whilst her other hand played with my tits, and then she withdrew her fingers as she slid to her knees and lifted my skirt and before you could say Jack Robinson she plunged her head between my thighs and started to lick all around my swollen clitty.

'I held my legs open as wide as possible so that she could get her tongue further in, and I began to get carried away by all this licking and lapping and I cried out: "Oooh, that's so good. Ohhh, yes, flick my clitty with your tongue, ohhh!"

'Delia reached round my waist with her arms and gripped my bottom to force my pussy even tighter against her mouth. She was now also so aroused that she began to pant loudly and started talking between licks.

'"Oh Andrea, your juices are so sweet! I love sucking your cunt and I'm going to bring you off now," she groaned and I felt her palms digging into my soft bum cheeks to pull my spread cunny lips onto her eager lips and tongue. She slipped a finger between my buttocks and began rimming my arsehole with her forefinger whilst she ran the pointed tip of her tongue up and down my sopping cunny crack at the front.

'My pussy began to palpitate wildly and I threw back my head in ecstasy as she brought me off with her tongue. It was a fantastic orgasm and I had to sit there for a few minutes to recover my senses. I would have liked to have returned the compliment then and there by licking out Delia's pussy, but the cleaning staff were due in at any time and so I had to wait till the next day, when she came round here and we spent a lovely afternoon sucking and fucking each other.'

Andrea wrapped her fingers around Martin's prick and was delighted to feel the smooth, fleshy tube swell and bound in her grasp.

'M'mm, your cock's in good condition, but I think your body needs toning up, my dear, before we make love again. Did you know that I am a qualified masseusse? No? Well, turn over and lie on your tummy and I'll give you one of my special treatments,' she suggested and when Martin obediently settled himself down in the required position, she knelt between his legs and gave him a slow, sensual massage, starting at his neck and working all the way down his back, over his dimpled buttocks and down to his feet, surprising him by the strength in her hands.

'Lie slightly on your side,' said Andrea as she ran her fingertips ever so lightly down his spine – and this time when her fingers reached the small of his back, she slid her hands back and forth across his bum cheeks, then down the outsides of his legs, travelling back up on the inside of his thighs and softly caressing his cock and balls. Martin was lost in a whirl of sensation as her insistent fingers rubbed up and down his shaft until he gasped out that he would come if she didn't stop this sensual stroking.

Andrea smiled and ran her tongue hungrily over her lips. 'You men have so little will-power,' she complained as she pushed Martin over onto his back, and slowly her tongue licked its way down his body, stopping at the nipples and his belly-button before her lips closed over the wide, broad column of his cock. He shuddered as her tongue flicked over his knob, down the shaft and over his balls before reversing the route back to the mushroom dome. Her moist mouth worked over every inch of his rock-hard stiffstander, her hand grasping the base as she pumped her head to and fro, keeping her lips taut as she kissed and sucked his palpitating prick.

Martin felt his balls tighten as she sucked juicily on his smooth, rounded knob which slid along the roof of her mouth to the back of her throat. Andrea sensed

194

that he was about to come and started to swallow just before the first spurts of jism came crashing out of his cock, and she gulped down all of the sticky seed from his twitching tool which was still erect as Andrea pulled her head away and flipped herself over onto her belly.

He slicked his hand up and down his stiff shaft which was still wet from her saliva as he surveyed her creamy smooth buttocks, the wrinkled little rosette of her arsehole and the glistening pink slit of her pussy pouch between the wide-spread cheeks, and the thought flashed across Martin's mind that he needed a snooker champion to tell him whether he should go for the pink or the brown!

Andrea must have sensed his dilemma for she turned her head and whispered: 'Stick your fat cock up my cunt, Martin, I'm not into bum-fucking!'

'Whatever you want, my dear,' he said reassuringly and her curvy body trembled as Martin carefully pulled apart the delectable cheeks of her bum and slid his pulsing prick through the crevice, sinking his cock into her dripping cunny in one smooth thrust. She was so wet that his shaft was coated with cuntal juice as soon as he began pumping his rigid rod in and out of her juicy honeypot. The hairs on his chest brushed against her back as his veiny truncheon slipped in and out of her dripping crack.

She felt behind her until her fingers found the dark, hairy crack of Martin's bum and then she fondled his hairy ballsack, holding it in her hand whilst they fucked happily away in perfect unison. Her superb, pear-shaped backside responded to every one of his pistoning shoves and Martin now snaked his arms round to fondle her big, tawny nipples as he drove home again and again, exciting her to such raging peaks of lust that she cried out: 'More! More! Quicker now, Martin! Give me all you've got! I want you right up to your balls!'

Andrea and Martin were now at fever pitch and they both tensed up at the approach of their oncoming orgasm. Martin's cock quivered when Andrea ground her bottom against his thighs and with a low growl he shot his load, creaming her cunny with his hot, frothy seed as she waggled her bum from side to side, shuddering with ecstasy whilst the force of her own climax swept through her body.

Martin collapsed down upon her and they lay in a tangle of limbs until Andrea reached out and pulled the duvet over them. 'Goo'night,' said Martin sleepily as she switched off the light and in less than a minute they were both fast asleep.

This was more than could be said for Debbie, Cable's young receptionist who had spent the evening with her girlfriend, Barbara, because although she and Craig Grey had kissed and made up earlier in the evening, Craig could not disguise the fact that he was suffering from a bad headache and Debbie insisted that he went home and had an early night.

'I want you to be in good nick for our early morning fuck tomorrow,' she told him firmly. 'And besides, I'll now have a chance to see Barbara Thomas who's staying with her auntie in London tonight,' she told him firmly. 'We were best friends at school, but we don't have the chance to see much of each other these days because she's now living near Luton and only comes up to town occasionally.'

So, during the evening, Barbara and Debbie enjoyed a Chinese meal and a long gossip and, later on, neither Debbie's parents nor Barbara's aunt made any objection when Barbara asked if she could stay the night with Debbie. They hauled a divan into Debbie's bedroom and after polishing off the half bottle of vodka which Debbie had smuggled in from the off-licence, the two girls began to exchange confidences about their love lives.

'I'm going out with a very nice guy named Peter,' Barbara confided to Debbie as they sat together on the divan. 'He's much older than us, nearly thirty, and he's the deputy manager at the supermarket where I work. He's not married and although he's nice-looking he's very shy. I knew he fancied me because he was always finding excuses to talk to me when I was working but he never plucked up the courage to ask me out, so I had to be forward and make the first move!

'Peter drives this lovely big Rover three-litre car, and one afternoon whilst we were chatting in the canteen I asked him straight out if he would take me for a ride in it one day after work. He blushed as red as anything and said: "Yes, of course, let me give you a lift home tonight."

'Peter was so shy that I had to suggest that he took me out for a drink the next night and he was a perfect gent and didn't do anything except give me a peck on the cheek at my front door when we got home. But on the next date Peter showed me that he wasn't *that* shy! After going to the films he drove out to his tennis club car park. It was all dark and quiet and I could see that Peter was trembling slightly when I suggested that we climbed into the back seat. Still, once we were snuggled up together we soon had our arms around each other and it felt very good.

'He began by kissing my cheek, my lips and then he moved slowly down to my neck. His tongue was flicking over my skin and I heard him catch his breath when he caught sight of my erect nipples which were pushing up against the silky material of my blouse. We began to French kiss and I started to be really turned-on. When his hand reached inside and cupped one of my tits, and he rubbed my nipples whilst lifting my breasts up and down, I could feel my panties getting sticky.

'My pussy was aching for attention and so I pulled Peter's hand to my knee and flung open my legs as his fingers sidled up to my crotch and pulled off my wet knickers. He stuck his thumb inside my cunt and finger fucked me till he brought me off.'

Debbie was listening intently as she sat on the bed, hugging her knees whilst she listened to her friend's confession. 'Was he a good fuck?' she enquired. 'Older men might not be able to screw all night, but if they're more experienced that often more than makes up for it.'

Barbara looked hurt and she smacked Debbie lightly on her leg. 'Shame on you, Debbie Howard! I wasn't going to let Peter fuck me on our first date. What sort of a girl do you think I am? But of course it wouldn't have been fair not to let him come so I decided to give him a wank – and that's when things went a bit haywire!'

'Don't say he tried to fuck you by force!' said Debbie, aghast at the very idea of her friend being at the mercy of a sex-crazed man.

'No, nothing like that,' responded Barbara quickly. 'I told you that Peter was a gentleman – and if anyone tried that with me they'd get a swift kick in the nuts! But I'm careful when I choose which boys I'll go out with and I've never had any trouble with my dates. Perhaps it's because I make it plain just how far I'll let a boy go!'

'Anyhow, I broke off our kiss and said to Peter: "Look, I don't want to fuck but I'm going to give you some relief with my hand. Okay?"

'Oh yes, yes, thank you!' he groaned as I unbuckled his belt and pulled down the zip of his flies and I got my first shock of the evening! Peter was wearing a pair of tight blue briefs which were so small that his knob pushed itself up and over the top, and one of his big hairy balls had swung out of the elastic at the side. I bent forward and took hold of his pants and slowly rolled them down – and what a huge cock sprang up to greet me! Honestly, Debbie, I don't mind telling you that I've seen a few pricks in my time – do you remember the first ones we ever saw? It was when we were in the fourth form at school at the Christmas dance and we took Johnny Mitchell and Gerry Thomson outside and showed them our tits whilst they tossed themselves off – but Peter's was easily the thickest I'd ever seen!

'I had to hold his cock in both hands as I knelt

over him and as my boobs were bobbing through my unbuttoned blouse, I bent right forward and brushed the sides of his monster shaft against my nipples.'

'Sounds really super,' said Debbie with a wistful sigh as she let the fingers of her right hand stray between her legs. 'Just listening to you is getting me all worked up, you naughty thing.'

'Well, I was getting pretty excited myself,' Barbara admitted with a giggle. 'There's a lovely feeling of power when you know you've turned on a boy so much that he can't stop his cock sticking up whether he wanted it to or not.'

'And I take it that Peter didn't want to,' commented Debbie who was now fingering herself openly. 'Go on, Babs, what happened then?'

'What happened then?' her friend repeated with a hollow laugh. 'I got the shock of my life, that's what happened! There I was, giving Peter a lovely slow wank when by pure chance I lifted my head for a second and I saw that we had a Peeping Tom watching us from behind a tree only a few yards away! He was only a kid, probably about fifteen or sixteen, and my first instinct was to blurt out what I'd seen to Peter who was flat on his back, moaning with pleasure as I slid my hand up and down his giant pole.

'But then I thought, what the hell, I could see how entranced the boy was, his eyes wide open with excitement, his mouth hanging open and, as he moved slightly, I could see that he was jacking off. He hadn't noticed that I'd spotted him and I decided to give him a five-star show. So to Peter's surprise and utter delight,

I stooped down and rolled my tongue all over his wide purple helmet. I gripped his shaft by the base and licked and lapped all over his veiny length and I cupped his tight-stretched balls in my hand whilst I swirled my tongue all over his knob.

'Peter's prick twitched in my grasp and when he began moaning I knew he was about to come and just as he spunked, I pulled his cock to the side and a thick splodge of jism shot across the interior and splattered against the very window the young guy was looking through! What with the window being already rather misted up from our breath, Peter's cum now completely covered us from the gaze of our voyeur and it was with some relief as well as amusement that I heard his footsteps scurry away.'

'Did Peter hear anything?' enquired Debbie, who was now openly sliding her finger up and down her love crack over the material of her panties.

'No, not a thing, he was too busy moaning and groaning as I finished sucking him off, and I wasn't going to tell him anything for it might have upset him to discover someone had watched us playing with each other. As my mum says, what you don't know won't hurt you and the lucky beggar got far further than he would have done if I hadn't seen the Peeping Tom!'

Barbara paused and then moved across to Debbie and softly added: 'Here, Debbie, would you like me to give you a helping hand?'

'Yes please,' panted the other girl who threw herself back and arched her bottom upwards so that Barbara could wrench off her sodden knickers.

'Oooh, you're so soaking wet down there,' said Barbara as she screwed up the saturated panties and made a sheath for her forefinger with the fine, well-moistened material before rubbing it firmly on Debbie's sopping slit. This made the lithe girl's body twist and writhe and when she inserted her finger to the hilt inside her juicy cunt, Debbie heaved herself up and down with wild abandon at this sexy frigging and her body shivered all over whilst waves of climatic electricity spread out from her crotch.

When these finally subsided, Barbara withdrew her finger and threw the drenched panties to the floor as she snuggled her head between Debbie's creamy thighs and buried her lips in the soft hairs of her wispy, auburn bush. Momentarily she drew back to flick her tongue over the hard nub of Debbie's clitty and she felt the shock waves of her caress ripple through Debbie's body.

Almost of their own volition, Debbie's legs splayed wider as Barbara's tongue raked the erect little clitty which had popped out of its pod.

'Oh yes, Babs, eat me out! Ooooh, that's groovy!' cried out Debbie and Barbara now began to play with her in earnest, sucking open-mouthed and rolling the long lips of Debbie's cunny between her own before plunging her tongue deep inside her pussy. She slurped noisily on Debbie's honeypot, delighting in the tangy aroma which wafted into her nostrils, and Debbie's hips thrust urgently up and down to draw her fleshy clitty further inside Barbara's mouth whilst the girl lapped up the love juices which were now freely flowing from Debbie's cunt.

Barbara felt Debbie's climax building up as her fluttering tongue darted in and out of her hairy quim, and she worked her tongue even harder until Debbie howled with joy as she came in great shuddering spasms.

When they had recovered, Debbie was ready and willing to continue but they were now quite sleepy and as both of the girls had to get up early in the morning, Barbara switched off the light and they simply cuddled up together. Within minutes they were both fast asleep.

On the dot of seven o'clock the next morning, Ivor was woken out of a pleasant though improbable dream in which his beloved Fulham were beating Manchester United by five goals to nil by the insistent buzz of the alarm on Mandy's bedside radio. Mandy yawned and as she stretched out her arm to silence the alarm she murmured: 'Time for you get up, Ivor. You'll have to whizz back home to change before you go to work.'

He nodded and Mandy snuggled down again and closed her eyes. 'Hey, what about you?' said Ivor, gently shaking her by the shoulder.

'Oh, I've got the morning off,' she replied sleepily. 'I'll pop into the office for an hour or so after lunch and then three of us are going up to Manchester this evening. We have an important presentation to make for one of our top clients, so we'll spend the night in Manchester and be fresh for the fray tomorrow morning.'

Ivor groaned and slid his feet out of the bed, placing

them on to the floor. He hoisted himself up but then he lifted the quilt and his already semi-erect shaft stiffened up into a pulsing stiffness as he gazed upon Mandy's nude body curled up in a ball. Although he knew that Martin Reese wanted to see him first thing this morning, the sight of Mandy's soft, rounded bum cheeks sent all thoughts except making love to this beautiful creature scurrying out of his mind.

He hurriedly slipped back into bed and rolled the delicious girl onto her back, and she reached down and grasped his anticipating prick. 'Ivor, I'd love you to fuck me but I don't want you cursing me later if you find yourself in trouble at work.'

'I'd never do that,' he mumbled as he planted a quick series of little kisses on her rising nipples, nibbling one brown tittie and then the other, making Mandy squirm in ecstasy as she continued to slide her fingers up and down his throbbling tool.

With a growl, she twisted away and scrambled up to straddle him, sitting on his thighs as she pressed his thick, rampant, rod into the soft folds of her pussy. Then Mandy lifted herself up and mounted him fully, sliding his shaft between her cunny lips as she ground her hips down, swaying from side to side so that Ivor's delighted cock was totally enfolded in her moist, clinging honeypot.

'Lie back and enjoy yourself,' she advised him as she bounced up and down on his boner, and Ivor lifted his hands to cup her jiggling breasts. 'As I don't have to get up till eleven o'clock, I'll do all the work.'

He was more than happy to comply and he lay on his

back with his eyes closed whilst Mandy rode him like a jockey in the Grand National. Savagely, she thrust herself down upon his tingling tool and Ivor was soon swept up in her rhythm and began to jerk his hips upwards in time with her downward plunges so that his prick rubbed sensuously against her clitty. They rocked together in unison and when Ivor's cock began to twitch and his body began to go rigid, Mandy sensed that he was about to climax and she slammed down hard on his shaft, twisting her thighs around his rib cage, clamping his cock deep inside her as the force of his sticky jism ignited her own orgasm and she shivered with pleasure as her body shivered its way to an exciting pinnacle of pleasure.

Perhaps because he had been more passive than usual in their lovemaking, Ivor was pleased to find that he could still carry on with this delicious fuck. Without taking his still stiff prick out of Mandy's dripping crack, he rolled her over on to her back and their mouths locked and they kissed hungrily, their tongues wiggling wildly in each other's mouths. Mandy twined her legs behind his back, locking her ankles together, and Ivor whimpered with pleasure as he slid his hands underneath and fondled her firm backside as he swung his cock deep into the delicious love channel between her legs.

This time Mandy was the first to come and she gasped: 'Keep going, darling, I'm almost there! Just keep working your lovely big cock in and out of my cunt, you randy sod! Faster, now, faster, I want you to spunk inside me again!'

They fucked like a fury and Mandy pulsed with pleasure as Ivor plunged his stiffstander in and out of her squelchy slit with increasing speed. Mandy came first, this time with a long, sustained moan that rang out through the flat, and Ivor's groans mingled with hers whilst she twisted and bucked as the two of them shuddered the course of a tremendous orgasm.

She clawed at his back as Ivor's cock crashed into her one last shattering time, and his brawny frame shuddered violently as he spurted his spunk inside her sated pussy, and the couple lay panting as ripples of bliss flowed through their bodies.

They lay quietly together for a few minutes until Mandy tapped him on the shoulder and said generously: 'Go on, Ivor, pop into the bathroom and take a quick shower and I'll put on the kettle and we'll have a bite of breakfast before you leave.'

In his luxurious suite in The Cranbrook Hotel, Bennie Hynek was also in the shower although his partner for the night, the nubile blonde receptionist whom he had chatted up when he had returned to the hotel from the lavish lunch provided by Cable Publicity, was still asleep in the big, king-sized bed. Since tumbling on to the crisp cotton sheets shortly after midnight they had made love three times, but Bennie was an inveterate early riser and shortly after seven o'clock he had slipped quietly out to go into the bathroom.

Hotel rooms made for wonderful sex, Bennie said to himself as he turned off the tap and wrapped himself inside a thick white bath towel. A room in a four star city hotel was always comfortable and yet would always be impersonal enough to allow a guest to let down his hair – after all, he is not at home and feels free to do things that would leave the stain of guilt in his own bedroom.

Certainly, he would have been unable to offer Jackie a bed for the night back home – Tanya, his live-in girl-friend, would have something to say about it for a start! So there was all the more reason, how did the English put it, to make hay whilst the sun shines. As he dried himself the door opened and Jackie stood naked in front of him.

'Hi, Bennie, have you showered already? I'll follow your example,' she said brightly, kissing his cheek as she made her way to the shower. She did not draw the curtain and the Israeli looked at the pretty girl with an ever-growing interest surging through him as she let the fierce jet of water course through her short blonde hair.

Jackie's body was perfectly defined. Her breasts were large, heavy and tawny-nippled and when she lifted her arms and put her hand up behind her hair, her bosoms rode smoothly up her rib-cage. Her stomach was not flat but smooth and pure white, curving down softly in a classic line to her pussy which was initially covered by soap, but when she allowed the water to wash the soap away, Bennie caught his breath at the sight of her silky, flaxen muff inside which peeked through the long pink lines of her cunny lips.

Wordlessly, he folded his towel back on the heated rail and joined Jackie in the shower where he took the soap from her hands and began lathering her alabaster white skin. He massaged the rigid nipples between his thumb and forefinger and she let out a high-pitched moan when he began to wash her pussy. He rubbed lightly around her mound at first, letting his fingertips go near but never touching her throbbing clitty.

'Ohhhh! Ohhhh! Ohhhh!' Jackie moaned as she writhed in ecstasy as Bennie began to frig her skilfully, pressing his open hand against her bottom and then drawing his hand forward to let two of his fingers rise between her pussy lips to meet her erect clitty which he massaged delicately as she gyrated her hips against his hand until she was on the brink of an orgasm.

Then he backed her against the wall and, going down on his knees, he licked and lapped her pussy and his tongue found its way through the sopping silky strands of pubic hair and lashed her soft cunny lips.

Jackie's love juice now dribbled like honey out of her cunt and he tickled her erect clitty with his darting tongue, and she panted with pleasure as the aromatic cuntal liquid flowed over Bennie's face. She screamed as he brought her off with his tongue, sucking hard on her clitty until she shrieked with joy as she achieved her climax.

Bennie scooped her up in a towel and carried her into the bedroom where he lay her on the bed. She spread her legs and slid a pillow under her cute little bottom, then thrust herself forward so that her pussy was jutting out, almost begging to be fucked.

Jackie reached out and grasped his rock-hard shaft and said brightly: 'What a luscious looking cock! I must say that circumcised dicks always look clean and stripped for action.

'To be fair, though, my boyfriend washes underneath his foreskin every day and once his prick's on jack there's no difference between his and yours as far as I'm concerned,' she added as she gently fondled the length of Bennie's thick, eight-inch prick.

Without further delay he positioned his cock between her thighs and rubbed his knob against her moist pussy lips. Her breathing quickened and her legs began to tremble as he rammed his rampant stiffstander up her tight, juicy cunt in one push. Jackie let out a tiny whimper as he pumped into her furiously and thrust herself against him with each stroke. He drove home again and again as the quivering girl urged him on, closing her feet together at the small of his back to force every inch of his pulsing prick inside her. He sucked on her raised tawny nipples as he pistoned his prick inside her sopping love channel, reaming the far walls of her cunny as their pubic hairs matted together.

Jackie slid her hand forward to fondle his balls and this sent Bennie over the top. With a hoarse cry he drenched her cunt with a tremendous jet of hot, frothy jism as her soft body quaked underneath him.

'Damn it, I've come too quickly,' panted Bennie and the thought flashed through his mind that he should have dabbed a coating of *Stallion* on his tool before he began this delicious fuck. 'I'm sorry, Jackie, I know you haven't come – but lie back and I'll finish you off by eating your pussy.'

'How lovely,' murmured Jackie as she settled herself

down on her back as Bennie pressed his hand upon her soaking mound, letting his fingers play around in the silky bush of corn-coloured hair. She moaned softly as he slid one long finger along the edges of her red chink, and when he slid a knuckle inside her cunt she pushed herself upwards, arching her back and wriggling her body as if to signal that he should penetrate deeper inside her sopping gash.

Bennie's mouth now bore down on her erect titties, flicking the tawny flesh expertly with his tongue whilst his finger slid in and out of her cunt. Jackie gasped as she felt her clitty popping through her cunny lips as Bennie's lips and tongue now travelled downwards, nipping, licking and nibbling at her skin and, when he reached her belly-button, her whole body arched upwards as he now rubbed her clitty with his thumb, making it protrude like a tiny cock as he parted the blonde strands of her fluffy muff with his fingertips and pressed his lips against her cunt, which made her yelp with delight as she threshed around and clamped his head between her thighs.

He could taste the tangy mix of Jackie's cuntal cream and his own salty spunk as he let his tongue work all over her clitty, and then he let it delve deeper into the juicy wet crack of her cunt. Pushing his mouth up firmly against the yielding lips of her cleft, Bennie began to move his head back and forth along her juicy slit as he lapped up the tasty cocktail of their sex juices which were now flowing freely out of her honeypot. With each stroke of his tongue she cried out in ecstasy and he could feel her clitty expanding and her legs begin

210

to shake as she drummed her heels on his chubby buttocks.

Then Jackie relaxed as Bennie's warm tongue prodding through her cunt sent the feel of a delightfully warm, enveloping orgasm spreading through her body, and she pulled his head away and they lay together side by side. She slicked her hand up and down his cock which was now as hard and stiff as she could wish, and she nimbly hoisted herself down to kiss and lick Bennie's hairy ballsack whilst she continued to massage his pulsing shaft.

When she judged his shaft to be at its peak, Jackie swiftly turned over onto her belly and pushed out the firm white cheeks of her peachily rounded backside towards Bennie's glowing face. He bent down and kissed each cheek in turn as she turned round and watched him fumble for the drawer in his bedside table where he kept a tube of *Stallion*.

'What's that stuff?' she asked as Bennie squeezed out a generous amount of the orange cream from the tube and rubbed it all over his cock.

'Just some stuff to make my prick slide in easily,' said Bennie as he pulled a pillow towards them and slipped it under Jackie's stomach.

'Oooh, are you going to fuck my bum?' she asked him, and Bennie chuckled as he replied in his best English accent: 'So long as you have no objection, my dear.'

'No, that would be rather nice,' said Jackie as she wiggled her delicious bottom, and Bennie inserted his prick in the crevice between her bum cheeks, pushing forward until the tip of his knob was at the entrance of her puckered little arsehole. The sticky cream on his shaft enabled him to push in three inches of his chunky cock, whilst one of his hands snaked under her arm to tweak her nipples and the other moved further down into her flaxen thatch to massage her clitty.

'A-a-h-r-e!' breathed Jackie as he pushed his sturdy shaft further forwards until she was corked to the limit, and she spread her cheeks further as he plunged his prick in and out of the narrow orifice. Bennie's cock filled her completely as he jabbed his twitching tool inside her bumhole, cushioning his stomach against her pliant buttocks and stretching her rear dimple to its fullest extent as he sawed in and out of her bum, rubbing her tits along his palm and the inside of his arm and stroking the hard nub of her clitty with the fingers of the other hand.

'I'm coming!' she shouted and with a cry of 'So am I!' Bennie flooded her bum with three fierce spurts of spunk. He lay on top of her, being careful to keep his throbbing tool deep inside her until his shaft began to soften, and then he pulled out and they held each other quietly as they recovered their composure whilst cuddling each other on the now very damp sheet.

They lay panting, wet from their shower and their fucking, and then Jackie planted a gentle kiss on Bennie's neck and said: 'That was a super screw! What was that stuff you smeared on your prick, Bennie? It lubricated me beautifully.'

'It's called *Stallion*,' replied Bennie. 'And not only

does it make my fucking more enjoyable, with any luck it's going to make me a rich man!'

He explained to her about *Stallion*'s miraculous properties which would prove such a blessing for the over-eager male, and Jackie nodded her head and said: 'Well, if it really does work, you're certain to make a fortune. But all I'm interested in now is whether we can coax your cock to perform one more time,' she added with a wicked glint in her eye.

He passed his hand across his forehead. 'Phew, I think you're a little optimistic,' he observed as Jackie slicked a dollop of *Stallion* cream on her hands and proceeded to slide them up and down Bennie's limp shaft, and he watched with growing interest as she licked around the thick, dark curls of his pubic bush and pressed her cheek against his shaft before moving her lips across to kiss his knob.

'Ah ha, we have lift-off!' said Jackie brightly as Bennie's prick began to stiffen and swell in her hand. 'Bennie, as soon as the first consignment of *Stallion* arrives in London, put me down for a dozen tubes!'

Bennie gulped hard as the lovely young girl started to suck lustily on his erect cock and, as he summoned up his last remaining reserves of energy, he wondered for the first time in his life whether it really was true that one could have too much of a good thing!

Also in the series

☐	0 671 71766 9	The Mini Mob	£4.50
☐	0 671 71767 7	Private Relations	£4.50
☐	0 671 71768 5	Public Affairs	£4.50
☐	0 671 71769 3	Coming Through the Rye	£4.50

These books are available at your local bookshop, or can be ordered direct from the publisher. Just fill in the form below.

Price and availability subject to change without notice.

SIMON & SCHUSTER CASH SALES,
PO Box 11, Falmouth, Cornwall TR10 9EN

Please send cheque or postal order for the value of the book/s, and add the following for postage and packing:

UK including BFPO - £1.00 for one book, plus 50p for the second book, and 30p for each additional book ordered up to a £3.00 minimum.

OVERSEAS INCLUDING EIRE - £2.00 for the first book, plus £1.00 for the second book, and 50p for each additional book ordered. OR Please debit this amount from my Visa/Access/Mastercard (delete as appropriate)

CARD NUMBER ☐☐☐☐☐☐☐☐☐☐☐☐☐☐☐☐☐☐

AMOUNT £ .... EXPIRY DATE ....

SIGNED ....

NAME ....

ADDRESS ....

....